Rachel and Adam Discovery

by

Jenna J Stanton

Copyright Jenna J Stanton © 2021

The right of Jenna J Stanton to be identified as the author of this work has been asserted in accordance with the Copyright, Designs and Patents Act 1988

First published in the UK in 2022

ISBN 13: 9798841849063

This book is sold subject to the condition that it shall not, by way of trade or otherwise, be lent, re-sold, hired out or otherwise circulated without the author's consent in any form of binding or cover other than that in which it is published and without similar condition including this condition being imposed on the subsequent purchaser.

Every effort has been made to fulfil requirements with regard to reproducing copyright material. The author will be glad to rectify any errors and omissions at the earliest opportunity.

There are millions of people out there who enjoy spanking and find the subject either erotic or cathartic. I dedicate this book to those who have thought about it, but never tried.

Jenna

x

Contents

1. A chance meeting
2. Back to reality
3. Adam De Vere
4. Rachel Lisa Delaney
5. At Angela's
6. Lunch in Covent Garden
7. So THAT's what it's like
8. The Aftermath
9. Business is Business
10. Back in London
11. In Amsterdam
12. Time for the Plan
13. Now the Waiting
14. Saturday
15. The Call
16. Angela's secret
17. Back at the restaurant
18. Angela plays out her secret
19. Eventually it's the Weekend
20. Alone at last!
21. There was still the weekend
22. Planning Rachel's Birthday
23. The gift
24. Angela and Jane again
25. Surprise
26. Dinner in Paris

27. Home to Face the Music
28. Discomfort
29. Planning the holiday
30. Arriving
31. Surf and Steel Bands
32. The Conversation
33. The rest of the Holiday
34. Angela and Jane catch up
35. The Solutions for Rachel
36. The Nitty Gritty
37. Tying up Loose Ends
38. Rachel leaves work
39. Jane Gets a Match

Chapter One

A Chance Meeting

Adam leant into the gusting wind and rain as he walked the few steps from his car to the restaurant.

"I'll make my own way home, Michael. Take the rest of the evening off", he shouted over his shoulder to his chauffeur, hoping he could be heard above the howling gale.

The chauffeur mock saluted his boss to acknowledge that he had. Once he had seen Adam shake his brolly and open the door to the restaurant, he slipped the Bentley into 'Drive' and smoothly pulled away from the kerb. It wasn't even eight o'clock yet and he looked forward to a lazy evening in front of the TV. They didn't come along very often.

The calm of the restaurant with its elegant furnishings, spaced out tables and soft music was a very welcome contrast to the foul weather outside.

"Good evening Mr. De Vere". The head waiter rushed to greet him. Adam was a good tipper. "Would you like your usual table?"

"Yes please Alfonse" replied Adam. "There will be two of us dining tonight. When Ms. Henderson arrives, please show her to the table."

Adam followed Alfonse to the table and thanked him as his chair was pulled out for him. He ordered a gin and tonic and sat back to await the arrival of a lady he had never actually met.

They had met in an online chatroom for people who enjoyed a particular – shall we say at this stage – interest.

Angela Henderson, apparently, shared his interest. At first, they had just swapped messages. Finding out a little more about each other's everyday life.

She was ten years younger than Adam's 38 and a strange sort of beautiful. Shoulder length brunette hair, slim build, green eyes, and a pretty smile

She was attracted to Adam's profile – athletic build, obviously a successful businessman, well dressed. He might be a keeper if things worked out.

Adam was equally attracted. Angela was pretty and she seemed fun, although he did hold back from telling her too much. You can never tell with these things.

As the 'relationship' grew, they swapped phone calls. Adam opened up a bit more about his work and is home, but Angela seemed strangely nervous, even after many lengthy calls.

Eventually they had agreed to meet, which is why Adam was seated in his favourite restaurant. It was in Chelsea and served Italian food – exclusive, but not too flash. He was hoping to impress. He relaxed as the time ticked on. They had arranged to meet at 8:15. Glancing at his expensive watch, he noted it was nearly that time now. Hmm.

He wasn't one for being nervous, but at 8:25 he was beginning to wonder if she had had a change of heart.

At 8:30 the door burst open, shattering the calm of the room. But it wasn't Angela.

Instead in walked a striking stranger. Blonde hair bedraggled, blue eyes, dressed in jeans and a blouse.

Her eyes scanned the room quickly and nervously. She was looking for a man on his own.

She very soon spotted Adam, who didn't know her at all. But she was undeniably a beautiful 'girl next door' type and Adam's eyes were transfixed as she walked straight over to him before a waiter could intervene.

"Adam? Adam De Vere?" she asked

"Yes….. what can I do for you Miss?" replied Adam.

"I've been asked to come here by Angela Henderson," said the stranger. "She's not coming and asked me to explain. Could you please spare a few minutes?".

Adam sighed. "Well, I guess I don't have much else to do" he said. "Please take a seat".

"Sure but let me straighten myself up a little please - it's blowing a hoolie out there!"

The stranger disappeared off to the washroom and re-appeared, slightly less bedraggled, a few minutes later.

Adam ordered her a drink.

"Now then" he said, "what's this about Angela being too afraid to meet me?". He smiled his easy smile.

The stranger smiled in return. "First things first, my name's Rachel Delaney. I'm a neighbour and a very good friend of Angela's"

She held out her hand which was gently shaken by Adam.

"Angela's a very shy person really. The bottom line is that she couldn't bring herself to come and meet a total stranger to talk about…..". Rachel felt herself blushing. "…. err…..um…. well, the sort of things people talk about on those sites", she finished awkwardly

"And what exactly would those things be, Ms. Delaney" responded Adam. He was teasing and she knew it.

"Um… well…. Stop making it so difficult!".

Angela had eventually confided in her about that site, but Rachel felt uncomfortable with talking about it with a stranger.

Rachel was more than a little shocked – this was staid, dependable Angela! She knew that many people enjoyed this particular sexual fantasy but had never experienced it herself and had no desire to. Other than that, Rachel had never really given it a passing thought.

By now Rachel was blushing heavily.

She tried clumsily changing the subject. "This is a lovely restaurant. Do you come here regularly Mr. De Vere?"

"Call me Adam, please" said Adam with a friendly smile. "Yes, it's a lovely place – good atmosphere, good food. I come here about once a week I guess".

"Listen, have you eaten?" he carried on smoothly.

"Actually no"

"Well why not join me for dinner? My treat"

"I'm not really dressed for a place like this"

"Nonsense! You look great. And I'd enjoy the company"

"Well.... ". She faltered.

"Please?" he asked with a disarming smile.

Rachel felt herself crumbling. Maybe it was the glass of wine. Maybe it was the fact that Adam was an imposing, attractive man who seemed good company.

"OK then. But one condition please?"

"Go on"

"I haven't been involved with... um... any of your special interests, so please don't steer this towards me having anything but a nice dinner with good company?".

"Rachel, I wouldn't dream of it".

He raised his glass. "You have to be into these things for it to be fun." They clinked glasses.

Rachel and Adam ordered three courses each with a bottle of fine Italian wine. They chatted and laughed their way through dinner and all too soon it seemed time to go home.

Angela would be anxiously waiting to know what happened.

"I'm afraid I've given my driver the night-off", said Adam. He asked for Alfonse to call her a cab home, insisting when she declined. "I've put this trip on my account, so please don't worry about the cab fare", he said

As they stepped out into the by now easing rain, Adam asked "I've really enjoyed this evening - could I please have your number, Rachel?".

"I don't think that's a good idea Adam, but it was a fun evening. Thank you".

"You're sure?"

"Yes, Adam. I'm sure", Rachel said confidently.

He sighed, resignedly, kissed her on the cheek, held the cab door open for her and waved her off into the foul night with more than a little regret.

Adam hailed a cab for himself before directing the driver to his large house in Surrey.

Two failures in one night!

He was losing his touch.

Chapter Two

Back To Reality

As Rachel's cab splashed through the still busy West London streets, she thought about the evening. About what an attractive guy Adam most certainly was.

About how assured and confident he was.

About Adam's easy charm and warm smile.

About how he was obviously well-to-do, without bragging about it.

About the fact that he had a driver for God's sake!

Maybe she been a bit hasty when she had refused him her number?

But then she remembered his 'little kink' and the fact that he'd most likely try to get her to go along with it if things were to progress.

So she put the thoughts to the back of her mind and began to concentrate on what she would be telling Angela when they met up in about 15 minutes from now.

Rachel had called her to ask if Angela would like her to come round so she could discuss how things had gone. It was quite late, but Angela didn't hesitate to say an emphatic 'Yes'.

The cab pulled up outside the 1930s semis dotted along the road in a West London suburb. Houses in Hillingdon were cheaper than some places, and the road she lived in was quiet and leafy. And affordable.

"Come on up" said Angela as Rachel leaned on the intercom. "I've poured you a lovely glass of red!".

Rachel climbed the two flights of stairs and was greeted by an excited Angela.

"Come on in" she beamed.

Hanging up her coat and gratefully accepting her wine, she began telling the story of the evening's events.

She didn't leave out any little details, even admitting that she'd refused to give him her phone number.

"Whyever did you do that?" asked Angela.

"I've decided I'm definitely not going to meet up with him, but there's no reason on Earth why you shouldn't", said Ange

"Hmm. Lovely guy, but I'm not into this fantasy. It's just not for me I'm afraid".

"Pah! If he's the catch you say he is, what harm would a good spanking do you? You don't know until you've tried, and you *might* even enjoy it"

"I don't think so! But thanks anyhow" answered Rachel a little prudishly.

She left after two glasses of wine to walk the short distance to her own apartment. She briefly thought about what Angela had suggested, but then put it to the back of her mind. She couldn't do such a thing.

Rachel was a beautiful girl and had plenty of male admirers. She had been in a relationship with Paul for twelve months or so, but things had got a bit stale, and they agreed to part about four months ago. There had been no one since.

Rachel slipped out of her clothes and caught sight of herself in the wardrobe mirror. She had a lovely figure and ran her hands over her pert breasts and smooth rounded bottom.

"Not bad" she thought as she slipped between the sheets to think about her evening.

If only they had met under different circumstances, then things might be different.

It had been a pleasant evening with a lovely man. She found herself absent-mindedly toying with the idea Ange had put in her mind for a little while and then dozed off into a fitful sleep.

Rachel woke early the next morning. Surprisingly, it was a beautiful sunny day with no sign of the rough weather the evening before.

She ate a breakfast of croissants and jam and went to the wardrobe to pick what she had ironed for work that day. After a long shower, Rachel slowly dressed, taking some time smoothing the creases out of the thighs of her tight skirt. Her thoughts began to wander back to the previous evening. Such a shame.

Rachel walked the short distance to the tube and then rode it to her place of work. Rachel was an Estate Agent. Enough money to keep her smart and solvent with the occasional night out.

She dreaded to think what last night must have cost.

"Stop thing about him for God's sake woman!" she kept telling herself.

But did she want to listen.

The next few weeks were really very busy at the estate agency. Plenty of property sales were generating a fair amount of commission and Adam faded to the back of Rachel's mind.

Faded, but never quite forgotten.

Rachel had been out for a few drinks with Angela, who teased her incessantly about Adam.

Rachel was quite short with her when she did this.

Perhaps Angela could see the cogs whirring in Rachels mind – something she denied vehemently. Rather too vehemently if you asked Angela.

Then there was the business trip to Leeds. A conference on techniques for presenting properties for optimising sales.

Rachel travelled up to Yorkshire and enjoyed the distraction of the conference. Hers was a national estate agency chain and she enjoyed meeting colleagues and putting faces to names she spoke to on the phone.

She found herself in a newsagent in a seedier part of the town, looking for a magazine which might interest her. Whilst looking, her eye was drawn to one of the top shelf magazines, boldly entitled 'Spanking and CP Monthly'. She was flustered, even though she didn't even pick it up.

Rachel hastily exited the shop, but her curiosity had been aroused. The picture on the front cover had grabbed her attention. Was this something she could endure or even enjoy? Might Adam enjoy this with her?

Going from the shop to a nearby pub, she ordered a large vodka and developed a plan. After another vodka, she brazenly marched back to the shop, picked up the magazine and paid for it, amazed at her own boldness.

She went straight back to her hotel and put the magazine in her room, ready to read later.

After dinner with her colleagues, Rachel could not wait to find out more from her magazine. She was excited all the way through dinner at the thought of it.

My God, was she really considering this?

Back in her room, she half undressed for bed and then, with trembling fingers, she picked up the spanking magazine.

Rachel stared at the cover picture for some time. It was of a girl, about her age, across a man's lap with her knickers around her knees. He seemed to be spanking her very hard and her face was contorted as he did so.

Rachel imagined herself over Adam's knee for discipline. That was the word they used, wasn't it?

She kept remembering Angela's words – "what harm would a good spanking do you?".

Was this picture one of a 'good spanking'? Would it result in sex after? Rachel was scared but transfixed.

Surely it would hurt like hell.

She decided, there and then, that she would talk to Angela about this in more detail once she got back to London and find out exactly what Angela's experiences had been.

Rachel read more from the magazine. She couldn't help herself. There were stories of naughtiness which was always punished. Of shoplifters and bad secretaries being taken in hand. Not just with spankings, but often with canings too.

Rachel was surprised to find herself highly aroused by the prospect of being properly taken in hand by Adam, like it or not.

She began thinking of all the naughty, mischievous things she had done recently which could earn her a first spanking. She quickly slipped her hand inside her pants and masturbated. She was amazed. It only took seconds before she found herself in the middle of the biggest orgasm she had ever experienced.

Wow! This was totally amazing. Who would've thought she would be craving discipline just few weeks after being introduced to the idea?

On the train back to London, Rachel called Angela's mobile...

"Ange? I'm on my way home. Can I come round and see you tonight please? About eight-ish?"

"Sure. What's so urgent Rach?"

"It's a bit embarrassing"

"Come on – you can tell me anything!"

"Did you honestly mean it when you said I should hook up with Adam?"

"Yes"

"And take a spanking?"

"Yes, if you'd like that"

"Well, I've decided it would be worth a try. I want to talk over everything with you. And I need to know how I'd contact him"

"OK, well I've deleted all trace of him from my computer, but I'm sure we can figure out a plan".

"Rachel?"

"Yes?"

"Make certain you are ready for this, you naughty, naughty girl! Hahahaha. See you later then

"I am 100% ready".

She hung up before adding quietly "I think".

Chapter Three

Adam De Vere

Adam De Vere worked in the often-unsavoury world of asset strippers. He would buy up companies and sell off any profitable assets – property, machinery, stock and so on – before closing down the company completely.

It often resulted in redundancies or cutbacks for people who had worked at the company for many years. Sometimes it was extremely difficult.

The rewards were high, and this was how he had made his millions so young. You had to be ruthless.

When he looked in the mirror, he saw a 38-year-old man, with the very first signs of greying at the temples. It made him look distinguished. He was undoubtedly handsome, and he kept himself in very good shape with regular gym visits and games of squash. He dressed expensively. Certainly, one of the very most eligible bachelors to ever have crossed Rachel's path.

Adam was born in Godstone, Surrey to extremely rich parents. His father, James, was a stockbroker in the city. His mother Jacqueline did a little charity work.

Sadly, they were both killed outright in a car crash. Both died instantly, which was some comfort. Adam was just 27 when this happened.

As he was an only child, Adam had inherited everything. The houses, the investments, the collection of vintage cars. Everything. He was worth many millions of pounds.

Suddenly, he was a very rich young man.

He had added to this fortune by developing his asset stripping business and was now worth billions of pounds. He owned properties all round the world and lived an extravagant lifestyle by any standards. His Surrey mansion alone was worth maybe £3 to 4 million. He been lucky but had worked and made many ruthless decisions to get where he was.

His thoughts wandered back to the night he and Rachel had enjoyed their impromptu dinner.

To her tousled blonde hair and her piercing blue eyes.

To her long legs and gorgeous figure.

To her tight jeans, stretched over her lovely bottom.

To her happy demeanour.

To her slight awkwardness and innocence about anything remotely sexual.

Adam knew there and then he would try to get in touch in the future. He was not used to being turned down.

But that would have to wait.

The next few weeks were going to be extremely busy for him. He had good intelligence on two companies which were ripe for his undeniable skills, and he had in depth research to do on them both.

One of the companies was in Northern Ireland and he quickly organised a visit to Belfast to open discussions. His private jet was in for a check and so he would have to use a commercial flight.

At the same time, he also expressed a desire to meet with the directors of the second company on his return.

That would keep him busy for a good couple of weeks.

Discussions in Belfast revealed that the company was ripe for asset-stripping, so Adam set the wheels in motion.

With all these hotel room nights, Adam found himself bored. He decided that he would have a bit of an online change.

The website he had used to meet Angela wasn't particularly fruitful. As with most of these sites, there was a huge number of men to women… and many of the 'women' were males just pretending in order to get their kicks.

He had been pleased when he met Angela, but hugely disappointed when she decided against a meet. Until, that is, Rachel turned up to explain.

He deleted his profile from the site and scoured the internet for a better site, reckoning on finding a paid for site where meetings were more reliable.

He found a couple of promising possibles but had had to put them to one side as his business took over.

But Rachel kept popping into his thoughts. At the most surprising times too.

On his return from Belfast Adam was in the closing stages of negotiating to buy the Irish company. It would yield a handsome profit if his plan to sell the factory units to Office space providers came good. He had found a buyer for the machinery too. It would mean making the staff redundant, but what was the saying about making an omelette without breaking the eggs?

The second company was in Birmingham. He confirmed his visit and drove up the next day. It transpired that many of the buildings weren't actually owned by the company and so things weren't as clear cut.

On investigation, the company would cost him more that the assets would realise and so he quickly backed out of any deal.

So, Adam drove himself back down the M40, M25 and back to his lovely home. Surrey was a lovely county with some not so lovely bits! Needless to say, his house wasn't in one of those.

Godstone was a beautiful, leafy village, yet still close to the M25 and Gatwick airport.

His car crunched to a halt on his long, gravelled drive. He smiled as he looked at the house, complete with tennis courts and swimming pool. Five acres of garden, eight bedrooms all with bathrooms. He had a snooker room too. What more could a guy ask for?

He tossed the keys on the table.

It was early afternoon by now. He'd maybe take a shower and change, then head off to the favourite restaurant where he could think about his last visit there.

Bloody Rachel. He couldn't seem to get her out of his head.

How *dare* she turn him down!

But Adam was used to getting his own way. Some of his previous girlfriends had said he was too controlling, but that was part of who he was so they could take it or leave it as far as he was concerned.

Rachel seemed somehow different. He was definitely going to try to find her again.

And soon.

Chapter Four

Rachel Lisa Delaney

Rachel Delaney was born 28 years ago in Wendover, South Buckinghamshire.

She was the daughter of middle-class parents, Esther, and Simon. Rachel had one elder brother – her only sibling.

Her dad worked in the accounts offices at High Wycombe hospital.

Her Mum worked part-time as a receptionist at the local Doctor's surgery.

She had had a sheltered upbringing – she went to a very good local school and breezed though her O and A levels, attaining 7 'O' levels and 3 'A' level passes.

Her parents were very conservative. They didn't discuss sex unless they absolutely had to. And they never swore. They went to church most Sunday morning's and avoided anything controversial.

Which explains why Rachel, despite her looks attracting lots of would-be suitors, was uncomfortable with talking about sex, kinky or not. It didn't stop her enjoying it, it was just that she was uneasy talking about it.

She left school and went to Surrey University in Guildford, studying academic subjects she was good at because she had no idea at all what she wanted as a career. In fact the careers advice she received at that time was pretty much non-existent.

She built up a modest amount of student debt. Not half as much as her peers, it seemed. But still significant.

And she eventually graduated and found herself still at a loss what to do with herself.

Her Dad, Simon, left home. It seems he was only hanging on until he saw his children through university. He had apparently been seeing a woman from work for years behind her mother's back. One day he just upped sticks and left. Rachel and her Mum were understandably devastated. Rachel decided to cut all ties with him, and he didn't make any effort to build bridges.

Shortly after, her Mum was diagnosed with a horrible, aggressive breast cancer. She had only weeks to live.

Rachel was heartbroken.

She liked to keep busy and so for a couple of years she took any old job for a while, before settling into work as a Chartered Surveyor at a local estate agency.

At first she rented and then, when at the Estate Agency bought, a modest flat in Hillingdon, West London.

It was a real struggle, but she just about kept up the repayments.

The house in Amersham had been sold when her Mum died, and Rachel was bequeathed some of the money. It paid for the deposit in Hillingdon. There was enough left to pay off her student loans and to furnish her new place. She was proud of herself.

She made a few friends at work, but was pretty much inseparable from Angela, who lived just a few doors away in the same road. They met one evening in the local pub. Both were sitting alone, and they just started chatting.

Angela was a refreshing change from her fairly dull existence! She swore like a trooper for a start. She talked openly about boyfriends. And sex with them. And the things she fantasised about. Turned out she had a spanking fetish and was looking for someone to try it out with.

Rachel was at first uncomfortable with this. After all she was from a background where swearing was frowned upon and anything other than missionary sex, once a week on a Saturday, was deemed kinky.

Anyhow, the pair got on like a house on fire and started meeting in the pub regularly. They enjoyed occasional lunches and nights out too.

Rachel had started seeing Paul. He was a really nice guy. Good looking too, but after nearly a year, Rachel tired of him. He seemed unable to make his mind up about anything. He was sexually un-adventurous. Rachel could see herself turning into her parents, and it was FAR too soon for that! She liked her men to be bad boys, despite that sheltered upbringing. Angela's ways must be rubbing off on her.

So she ended it with Paul.

She had been driving around in a bashed up Mini – the old version. It was a rust bucket and started costing her too much to fix, so it had to be scrapped. The final straw was when the door dropped off as she wound down the window at the traffic lights.

Rachel found herself changing. She swore a lot more for a start. That was definitely down to Angela!

And she, too, tried attracting a different, decisive type of man.

She couldn't find one though.

Bugger it.

Chapter Five

At Angela's

Rachel got home from work, showered, and changed into some comfortable jeans and a sweatshirt. The tight jeans showed off her long legs and shapely bottom.

Rachel stopped off at the off licence to pick wine for her visit to quiz Angela. She selected two bottles for the visit – she might need to be less inhibited for this type of conversation, even with her best friend!

Angela pressed the button to allow Rachel in and greeted her with a hug and a knowing smile.

"Well, well! Who would have thought this?" teased Angela

"Don't DO that!" retorted Rachel, irritated.

"Or what, you'll spank me?" said Angela, laughingly.

"Yes, I bloody well might!" a surprised Rachel replied. "And don't think I won't" she added for emphasis.

"Oh chill out Rach!"

"Well, what I'm considering is a huge step for me and I've come to you for help, not to be teased. You have experience in these things and you're about to get more than you bargained for if you don't help. I mean it. Perhaps that would help me get a feel for things, so I wouldn't get complacent If I were you."

Rachel had stunned herself. It had never even crossed her mind to spank Angela for her teasing. But she was asking for it. Let's see how it goes.

Angela went quiet, very quiet.

The two girls settled next to each other on the sofa.

"Right, I need to know some things before I move on with this. Will you help?"

"Try me"

"OK, some of the questions will be quite personal. Do you mind?"

"Not at all. It might even be fun" replied Angela.

Rachel cleared her throat and pulled out a list of scribbled questions.

Angela burst out laughing. "You made a LIST?"

Rachel ignored her.

"Have you ever been spanked or caned by a man?"

"Yes" was the answer. "Quite a few times for both"

"Good, thank you. Now did you meet strangers from a website for this or was it as part of a relationship?"

"Mostly as part of a relationship. You know how I like to tease and be sarcastic? Well one time my boyfriend had enough. He told me he was going to spank me, and I just laughed.

He grabbed my wrist and walked me to the bedroom. He sat on the bed and started unzipping my jeans. I couldn't believe he'd go through with it and just stood there incredulous. Not for long though.

He tugged my jeans down and bent me over his lap. I could feel his erection, so I knew it was turning him on. He explained that he was sick and tired of my sarcasm and that he was going to teach me a harsh lesson.

And then he pulled my pants down and started whacking me, really hard. He carried on for at least five minutes without stopping. I wailed and cried, but he wouldn't stop. After what seemed like an eternity, he stopped.

"NOW are you going to quit the teasing?" he asked.

"YES! YES!" I quickly replied, tears in my eyes.

"OK, you can sit up then".

I sat up and looked at him as if for the first time. My boyfriend had asserted himself and do you know what? I had enjoyed it.

Not the actual spanking, but the lying over his lap, the anticipation. And I found myself looking forward to the next time. Planning ways of getting him to do it again.

"I'm sorry" I found myself saying as I fondled his swollen penis and unbuttoned his trousers.

We had the best sex ever!"

"Wow" said Rachel. Those are exactly the sort of feelings I have been having! What about your first caning. Was it unbearable?"

"No, no. It was the same guy, about 3 or 4 months later. He had bought a cane and a paddle from a sex shop in town but had not used the cane as it was deemed only for very serious punishments.

On this particular day, I had borrowed twenty quid out of his wallet without asking, then gone to the pub and got a bit merry – well quite pissed actually.

When I got home, he was waiting. He asked me if I'd taken money from his wallet. I tried telling him I had just borrowed it until I could get to a cashpoint, but I couldn't get a word in. He could tell I was a bit drunk too.

"Right. This time you've gone too far. I'm going to take you into the bedroom and deal with you properly. Come on. Right now… and bring the cane.

"I was strangely compliant as I rescued the thickish cane from the cupboard and followed him into the bedroom. It was about as thick as a man's little finger. He had placed an armchair strategically. I was beginning not to look forward to this!

"Bend over the back of that chair" he ordered. I hesitated but did as I was told. I had earned this after all.

I bent over. The skirt I was wearing was flipped up over my back.

"A really good thrashing" I heard him mutter as he took my knickers down. "Are you ready?"

But he was angry. He didn't wait for the answer. He lifted the cane right up and began blistering my bum. Very hard. I cried and cried. I reckon he gave me 18 or 20 of the hardest strokes you can imagine.

And when he'd finished, I was a blubbering mess. A blubbering mess who couldn't wait for the next caning.

It's the anticipation before and the memories after a caning which are sexy and enjoyable. The actual thrashing is very, very painful but without it there wouldn't be any anticipation or memories. I slept on my front for 2 nights and the marks lasted almost 2 weeks."

"Wow!" repeated Rachel, a bit taken a back. "I have to say it sounds scary". But in her heart, she knew she was hooked. She would have to try this at least once. And she decided it should be with Adam. He made a mental note to meet with him again somehow.

Both girls sat quiet for a while, sipping their wine.

It was Angela who broke the silence.

"Rachel... were you serious about giving me a spanking for teasing you about Adam? Because telling you those stories have made me ever so horny and I do think I was awful to you..."

Rachel, a little worse for the wine, didn't hesitate. She stood up, looked Angela in the eyes and spoke. "Angela, until this is over, you will address me as Miss. Do you have a cane?".

"Yes Miss"

"Well, follow me to the bedroom immediately and bring it with you. I won't put up with your teasing and I intend to teach you a good lesson". Just like the story in her magazine

Angela, for now grinning, found the cane and did as she was told.

"Now, move that chair into the middle of the room. Somewhere I can get a good swing"

"Yes Miss"

Angela complied instantly

"Now take your jeans off".

"Yes Miss"

After removing her jeans, Angela was ordered to bend over the chair. Right over, on tiptoe.

Rachel picked up the cane and felt it's weight. She was unsure about this, but felt Angela somehow needed it, so she vowed to give it to her hard.

"You are going to receive 12 strokes, hard. Are you ready?"

"Yes miss" came the reply. "I am so ready!".

Rachel tried a few practice strokes in the air, and then lined up the cane across her friend's bottom. She lifted the cane back as far as she could manage and, after a pause, crashed it as hard as she could across the seat of Angela's knickers. Angela jumped a little, but otherwise didn't react. CRAACK! A second stroke landed right where the first one had. Rachel was not very accurate yet, but she'd get there. After about 30 seconds, Rachel unleashed the third stroke, then the 4th and 5th in quick succession. Angela squealed and jumped up.

"Get back over that chair now" ordered Rachel. You asked for this and you're getting it in full."

"One second. Before you bend back over, come here"

Rachel waited for Angela to comply and then said "Turn around"

Once Angela had turned, Rachel tucked the cane under her arm and then without ceremony, tugged Angela's knickers down to the floor.

"NOW, bend back over and don't you dare move, or we'll have to start again" (she had read that bit in a magazine story too).

Rachel set about completing her task, enjoying watching the vivid red stripes appear after each stroke. She really did go to town as she felt that was what Angela needed.

At last, the caning was complete, And Angela was told she could dress.

She stood up, very teary eyed. Rachel felt she had to give her a hug,

"It's over Angela. Don't do that again".

"No Miss"

""It's Rachel again now, Ange."

"Christ Rachel you really did a job on me there. I won't sit comfortably for a week!"

"Good. Perhaps a little more respect from now on?"

The girls smiled lovingly at each other.

"I want you to help me develop a plan please," said Rachel

"Let's get on with it then", said Angela.

So they did.

Chapter Six

Lunch in Covent Garden

Rachel and Angela didn't contact each other for a couple of days, which was unusual. Rachel broke the silence with a call.

They were both in central London on Friday and both were free for lunch. They arranged to meet at Tutton's in Covent Garden – an occasional haunt where the food was good and the prices good value

Both Angela and Rachel had said they wanted to talk about their feelings after their previous meeting.

Angela joked that she hoped the chairs were comfortable! Rachel took that to mean her bottom was still sore and felt a pang of guilt.

The sun shone brightly as Rachel walked through the Piazza to the restaurant. She walked in to see a smiling Angela already there.

At a table with comfortable seats. She smiled and waved as she was shown to the table Angela had reserved.

Angela half-rose and they hugged. It was a little awkward as they studied the menu and carefully chose their meals.

"How've you been, Ange?" asked Rachel.

"Sore!" laughed Angela.

"Yes, I wanted to talk about that. Shall I go first?" said Rachel.

"Sure, but don't feel too bad. I asked for it and by gosh I got it!"

"Well, I wanted to say that, whilst it was a great feeling of power and very satisfying to deal with your teasing, I don't think being the dominant partner in this sort of relationship is for me, really.

I've been thinking about this a lot and the idea of submission and punishment – letting myself go and trusting someone else enough to be under their control - is something which appeals and intrigues me.

But I'm so scared I won't be able to handle it when the time comes"

They talked in hushed voices so no one would overhear.

"Yes, I understand that totally", responded Angela. "It's something I feel too".

Rachel sighed with relief.

"I don't know exactly how to move this forward. I DO know that I want to spend time with Adam. And that I want to submit to his type of discipline.

"OK. How about this? You need to know what it feels like – EXACTLY what it feels like, to be properly punished. You want to submit to it, but you don't know if you'll be able to."

"So, what if, you come round to mine tomorrow, and I show you how it will be? It's the only way you can move on I reckon."

Just a complete one off, never to be repeated, but I will give you a good taste of what it will be like with Adam. How much it will hurt"

"Really?" said Rachel

"Really. Besides it will be an opportunity to get my own back! You'll be able to wimp out at any time without losing face to Adam" reasoned Angela.

Rachel paused thoughtfully before agreeing. "No caning though?", she pleaded.

"We'll see lady" came the reply. Without a smile.

Rachel felt a small shiver run down her spine. Angela had left her in no doubt that she meant business

Lunch had flown by and both girls had appointments in the afternoon.

"I'll text you a time later" said Angela formally. "I will tell you exactly what to wear. You will not be late. Understood?".

Rachel nodded dumbly and then Angela was gone. She had butterflies in her tummy now, she was going to find out exactly what this fantasy felt like. She was certain that Angela would deal with her properly and then she would know if this whole scenario was for her. If it was, she could plan for a meet with Adam. And if it hurt too much or didn't feel at all sexy, she could go back to her humdrum, everyday life.

This was exciting!

Rachel found herself daydreaming about the next day, to such an extent that she nearly stepped out in front of a Black Cab whilst walking to the tube.

"Wake up Missus!" shouted the cab driver.

"Fuck off" shouted Rachel, even though it was entirely her fault. She was surprised at her own language. Rachel hardly ever swore.

Hmm. Perhaps it was a good job Ange hadn't seen that, she thought!

She went directly home and started thinking about what was coming.

And how exquisitely panful tomorrow would be.

And smiled.

Just before she went to bed, the message pinged up on her mobile. She saw it was from Angela and her stomach turned somersaults.

She read it with a growing sense of anticipation.

"Rachel. I have thought about this a lot. We have arranged for you to have a taste of real discipline at 7pm tomorrow. It will be administered by me, and the rules are these:

1 – You will turn up at 6:55 pm

2 – You will be dressed exactly as follows:

Short, pleated tennis mini skirt.

Cotton blouse, well ironed

White satin or silk underwear

Flat court shoes

Any variations will result in additional punishment.

3 – Your hair will be tied back

4- From the moment you first address me, it must be like we are not friends. Like a visit to a real disciplinarian. From now on you will address me only as Ma'am until the punishment is over and you have left my flat

5- There will be no bottle of wine before we start and – once this is over – I expect you to leave, still addressing me formally (we will catch up on Sunday)

6 – You will confess any recent misbehaviour to me, looking me directly in the eye. Any errors or omissions which I find out about will result in very serious punishment. Do not even THINK of saying there has been no misbehaviour. There always is.

7 – Depending on what you say in point 6, you will be thoroughly punished with my choice of hand spanking, the strap, or the cane

8 - There will be no safe-word

9 – After the punishment, you will be made to stand in the corner with hands on head before you are dismissed

10 – I intend to deal with you very thoroughly. Tears and tantrums will result in extra punishment.

Do you fully understand and accept this punishment? If you confirm there will be no going back"

Rachel read the text time and again, mouth open. All of a sudden it seemed very real. Angela was being very strict with her.

But inquisitiveness had taken over. She HAD to know what it felt like. She HAD to know if she could withstand a proper punishment.

"Yes", she typed, her finger hovering over the 'Send' button. After a minute or two's consideration, she pressed 'Send'. There! She had done it!

A second or two later, Rachel's phoned pinged again. "Yes what?"

"Oops! Yes Ma'am. Sorry Ma'am"

"That will earn you one extra stroke of the cane tomorrow. Don't you dare be late."

Rachel gulped. She had hoped to avoid a caning. This was going to be serious.

Before jumping into bed, Rachel gathered together the clothes she would have to wear. She threw the pleated tennis dress and her best silk undies in the washer. She had a navy cotton blouse clean and ironed.

She hoped it would do. There was absolutely no doubt in Rachel's mind that she would be held to task if they didn't!

Ah well, it was too late now. Rachel was sure that Angela would invent some reason to deal with her harshly. That was the game, wasn't it?

And knowing this gave her a delicious sense of anticipation at what was to happen. She couldn't wait for this, painful as it would undoubtedly be.

Once again, her hand slipped inside her pants. This was becoming a habit.

A delicious one.

Chapter Seven

So THAT's what it's like

Rachel didn't sleep well at all. In her mind she kept playing through what was coming.

She tried hard to think of all her recent misbehaviour.

Definitely top of the list was telling the cab driver to fuck off.

She tried to come up with a list of very minor things for which she would not be punished severely. Maybe she'd have to not tell Angela about the episode with the cabbie!

Maybe she could turn up just a couple of minutes late. Maybe her blouse might be a little creased. Neither infraction should merit a thrashing like the one she administered to Ange.

She kept imagining her upturned bottom over Ange's knee, bared for a walloping. Or, even worse, over the back of Ange's sofa for a good dose of the cane.

She didn't understand why, but the thought of either really turned her on. Something she had never experienced was absolutely something she must try.

And how could it be better for the first time than with a friend? Or rather with Ma'am. She mustn't forget that, or she would be in more trouble.

Throughout the day the excitement grew to almost unbearable levels.

Rachel carefully ironed her bouse for the umpteenth time. She polished her shoes again.

And laid out the undies – the sexy lace ones in pure silk.

As time moved on and the time approached six o'clock. Rachel laid all her clothes out in her bedroom.

She showered and dried her hair, by now very nervous.

Rachel slowly began dressing for her punishment. She wished it was Adam, but she needed to find out how she would react first.

Finally, at twenty to seven, she looked at herself in the wardrobe mirror. She looked good – she knew that much. Her Golden hair shone. She glowed. Her eyes sparkled.

Rachel poured herself a large glass of wine to give her courage. White, just in case she spilled some on her skirt.

She didn't want this to be worse than she imagined. She coiffed it down and poured another one.

And then it was ten to seven. She slammed the door shut behind her and walked the few steps to Angela's flat. She stopped at the gate, looking up at the flat.

She gulped when she saw that the curtains were drawn, despite it being light until much later.

Should she go through with this? She was having doubts, but the thought of Adam spurred her on. She needed to know.

So, Rachel went down the short path to the front door. Hesitating for a second, she pressed the intercom button.

"Come up, Rachel" came the frosty response.

The door clicked open, and her legs trembled a little as she climbed the stairs.

No going back now, she told herself.

As she approached the door to the flat, it swung open.

Angela stood there, resplendent. She was wearing a tight-fitting black business suit with a loose-fitting top underneath. Her hair was tied back in a severe fashion. She looked stunning. And very much like she meant business.

"Come in here and lock the door behind you!", Angela ordered.

Rachel again shivered. Was it pleasure or was she scared? She decided it was probably a bit of both.

"You will not speak unless you are asked to, understand?" barked Angela. Rachel had never seen her friend like this.

"Yes Ma'am" she replied, thankfully remembering how to address her friend. It seemed alien.

"Right. Go and stand in that corner, face to the wall, while I finish preparing the room for your punishment."

Angela didn't need to say it twice. Rachel almost bounded to the corner.

"Face to the wall"

Rachel excitedly pressed her face to the wall.

"Good. Now wait"

Rachel had noticed that Angela had especially prepared for her visit.

The lounge was big, and the large sturdy table was now against the far wall. Rachel noticed immediately what was on it – a cushion and (she gulped) a leather paddle, a hairbrush, a leather belt. And the sturdy cane she had used on Angela only a few days ago. She was scared now.

The sofa, usually in front of the TV, was also pushed back against the side wall.

Rachel heard the scraping of further furniture moving and couldn't resist a peek over her left shoulder.

Angela noticed it immediately. "That will earn you another extra stroke of the cane", she said calmly. "When will you ever learn, Rachel?".

Rachel snapped her head round quickly and faced the wall.

Angela poured herself a glass of wine and went and sat on the sofa to enjoy it. Rachel was nearly wetting herself with excitement and anxiety as the minutes passed.

"Right girl. Here. Now!" barked Angela

A flushed Rachel approached her.

"Stand behind that chair there she pointed. Rachel noted a new chair had appeared towards the centre of the room.

She did exactly as she was told.

"Now, I think we'll start with my inspection. We'll see if your dress meets my approval".

Angela walked round Rachel, looking carefully for faults. She didn't find many.

"Not bad. But your blouse is a little creased. We'll inspect your lingerie in a few moments."

Angela walked round to face Rachel.

"So far you have earned three extra strokes of my cane", Angela began.

"No Ma'am, it's only two… One for not calling you Ma'am and…."

"SILENCE!... The third one was for the creased blouse and arriving 3 minutes late. And now you dare to speak when you haven't been told to. What are we to do with you?"

Rachel stayed silent this time

"Better, so as I was saying, so far you have earned four extra cane strokes. Anything to say about that Rachel?"

"No Ma'am"

Now, before we can begin, I'm going to ask you to own up to any misbehaviour recently. I want you to look me in the eyes – I can always tell when you're lying Rachel – and admit the behaviour to me. So?...."

Rachel couldn't look Angela fully in the eye. She was intending to lie about the Cab Driver and the swearing.

Angela walked up to her, slapped her face quite hard and grabbed her chin. She made her look directly in the eyes. "LOOK at me!".

Rachel was surprised. She was not used to this. But she obeyed.

"Well Ma'am, there are only a couple of things that I can think of. As well as the lateness and not ironing my top properly, in fact there is only one other thing...."

Rachel couldn't do this. She couldn't lie to Angela – she'd be found out straight away. And anyway, it would be sort of cheating.

"Go on..."

"Well, I don't know how to say this exactly. But on Friday, after I left our lunch, I was looking at my phone and walked straight out in front of a cab. The driver shouted at me. I swore at him Angela"

"Rachel! What exactly did you say? That's not like you at all"

Rachel swallowed hard. I shouted back at him. I told him to fuck off I'm afraid.

Rachel's eyes hit the floor, ashamed of herself.

God knows what this would mean for her backside!

"RACHEL!"

"I had previously decided you should be spanked, hard on your bare bottom. Then given four strokes of the cane, quite hard. The other items were for show.

You have earned four extras, so that would be eight quite hard strokes of the cane. But this changes things.

I need you to go back to the corner whilst I consider this. Do you have anything to say for yourself?"

"No Ma'am. I'm sorry Ma'am" was all Rachel could manage.

She went back to the corner to await her sentence.

A good twenty minutes passed while Angela considered the punishment.

"Right. Come back over here", said Angela eventually.

"Rachel, this punishment was meant as a taster, but you have taken it beyond that.

I am extremely angry with you. Now I will give you three choices.

You can either just take the taster punishment or you can take what you would get in real life for your disgusting behaviour, or you can quit now before it starts.

The taster punishment would be a spanking followed by 8 of the best with my cane.

The proper punishment – rightly deserved - would be a damned good spanking and 18 of the very best on your bare bottom, bent over that table. It is richly deserved, but you may decide you want out at this stage. I'm not here to brutalise you, but you may feel you have to know how you may be dealt with by a real disciplinarian, such as Adam."

Rachel burst into tears. She surely wouldn't be able to take that many, that hard!

"I will allow you fifteen minutes to decide. Your tears will make no difference to me I'm afraid. Go to my bedroom and think very hard Rachel. Come back in fifteen minutes with your decision.

Rachel snuffled out of the lounge to the bathroom. She washed her tear-stained face and then retired to Angela's bedroom.

What would she do? She was tempted to go home now and call it a day, but that way she would never know.

The taster punishment was a cop out, she knew, but it was probably manageable.

The thrashing was what she truly deserved, but seemed very harsh

She thought about Adam and came to a decision with a couple of minutes to spare.

Rachel walked unsteadily back into the lounge, amazed at what she was about to do.

"Stand up straight!"

She stiffened.

"Have you decided?"

"Yes Ma'am".

"Well, what's it to be then?"

"Ma'am, I will take the punishment I deserve. Thank you, Ma'am,"

"Well, I honestly think that's the correct decision Rachel. Just be aware that there will be huge weals and grazes on your bottom. You will be thoroughly caned if you go ahead.

Are you sure?"

Rachel hesitated…. "Yes Ma'am. It has to be authentic, and it has to be deserved. I feel this will be both.

Angela took her jacket off and went to the table. She picked up the heavy leather paddle and then went to the sofa. She sat on the middle cushion and indicated to Rachel to come over and stand on her right side.

Rachel, fearful of an even worse punishment did so immediately.

Without being asked, she placed herself over Angela's lap. She was on the verge of tears already, knowing the thrashing that was coming.

Angela was in no rush. She spoke almost gently to Rachel as she lifted the pleated with skirt high over her back.

"Very nice. At least you complied with the dress code" Angela said as she slipped her thumbs into the sides of the white silk briefs.

"These are too nice not to be on display, so for now I intend to start the spanking over your pants".

"Whatever you say Ma'am" said a terrified Rachel quietly.

"Indeed lady".

Angela smoothed her hand over the briefs and made sure they were tight across Rachel's lovely bottom.

Angela began spanking Rachel with regular swats on alternate bottom cheeks. They stung like hell, but Rachel knew she had deserved far worse. And she was about to get it.

And how right she was. After about 3 or 4 minutes, Rachel was made to stand up. Angela slowly, almost sensuously took her knickers down and then off completely.

Rachel felt vulnerable as she lowered herself back over Angela's lap. She was right to.

The spanking continued, harder now. Full strength slaps all over both sides of her bottom and the tops of her thighs. The tears flowed as Angela picked up the sturdy leather paddle.

"Now 30 with the paddle. You may want to grit your teeth for this".

Rachel could feel the smooth, cold paddle as it slid over her fiery cheeks. After a minute, Angela lifted the paddle and applied it with devastating effect. It hurt an awful lot and her bum was by now bright red. But Rachel managed to take it stoically and endure the full 30 strokes.

She cried, wailed even but she kept her position well. At last, this part of the punishment was over.

Angela bade her to go to the corner, hands on head, for ten minutes. Rachel needed a bit of recovery time, she knew intuitively. She was sobbing, her shoulders heaving, in the corner.

"In ten minutes, the caning will begin" said Angela almost heartlessly. "Prepare yourself".

And with that she left the room.

Rachel winced visibly as Angela re-entered the Lounge.

"Go and stand at the end of the table" Angela ordered.

"Now" she continued "I will offer you one chance to change your mind. You can either take the eight medium strength strokes from the taster punishment or else you can take the caning you undoubtedly deserve. Which is it to be Rachel?".

Rachel momentarily thought she had had enough, but it was at that moment she became truly submissive.

"I'll take the punishment I so richly deserve please Ma'am. I truly need to find out the consequences of my behaviour and I thank you for administering it without leniency".

"Very well, if, you are sure?"

"Yes Ma'am, I'm certain".

"Then bend over that table. Right over, so you are on tiptoe. You may use the cushion I have provided to lean on".

Rachel did as she was ordered. Angela walked behind her. She tapped the inside of Rachel's knees with the cane – an obvious hint that she wanted Rachel to adopt a legs slightly apart position. Rachel complied immediately.

She still had no knickers on from her paddling, but Angela tucked the cane under her arm as she carefully folded Rachel's skirt out of the way.

"Now grip on the sides of the table. Do not let go or else you will attract further strokes. Do not move Rachel. Understood?".

" Y-yes Ma'am," said Rachel. She was crying again now. It was fear. She vowed that she would take the eighteen strokes to finish the punishment without any fuss.

This is to be 18 of the VERY best Rachel. Let us begin.

Angela took up position behind and to the side of Rachel. She placed the tip of the cane in the middle of Rachel's bottom. She placed her left hand on her hip and began the caning.

She lifted the cane right back above her shoulder and cracked it down viciously on Rachel's backside. Rachel didn't feel a thing immediately, but after a second the most dreadful agony whipped across her bottom. It was on fire. Rachel screamed but managed to hold her position.

Angela watched with satisfaction as the first bright red mark appeared on Rachel's bottom.

She waited about thirty seconds before placing the cane on Rachels bottom, ready for the second stroke. Then she again lifted it and brought all her force to bear on the second stroke.

Poor Rachel was in agony but was absolutely determined to see this through. Her legs thrashed about as she was well and truly caned eighteen times. It became a little less painful towards the end, but she knew all about every single stroke.

The last stroke is always the hardest said Angela, who was thoroughly enjoying herself by now.

Rachel gripped the table hard, screwed up her sobbing eyes and waited.

THHHHWHACCCCK! Angela took a step up and put every ounce of her strength into that last stroke.

Rachel jumped up, almost screaming.

"Now go stand in the corner and think about this," said Angela.

Rachel saw no reason to disobey now.

She went to the corner and stood with her hands on her head. My God that had hurt. Angela was a vicious bastard, she decided.

She was crying continuously

Angela came up behind her and lifted her skirt to inspect the damage.

She ran her hands over the perfectly shaped bottom and felt the vicious dark purple cane marks. Rachel's whole bottom was marked to varying degrees. There were even grazes where the cane had landed more than once on the same spot. Bruises were coming out already.

Angela regretted how harsh she had been. This had gone a bit far.

Rachel was told she could go.

She dressed gingerly and was in floods of tears.

"You vicious, sadistic bastard!" she said to Ange.

"I didn't deserve that. I'm never trying it again and that is the end of our friendship".

"But Rach.", started Angela.

"Don't you Rach me! FUCK OFF YOU SADIST!".

And Rachel stormed out.

Not even bothering to slam the door.

Chapter Eight

The Aftermath

The short walk home proved painful. Rachel was still crying as she put the key in her door.

She went straight to the full-length mirror on her wardrobe and gingerly removed her pants. She almost daren't look.

Het usually soft, unblemished rear was bruised (she guessed from the spanking) and criss-crossed with angry purple welts with raised edges. Where the cane strokes crossed, there was the odd spot of blood. Rachel had found out exactly how bad it could be.

She did her best to apply antiseptic cream, but the pain made her bottom so uncomfortable to even touch lightly.

She decided that it was best to go to bed. She would be sleeping on her front for a few nights, that was for sure.

Rachel took off her clothes and slipped into bed. Even the weight of the quilt was hard to bear.

Gradually calming, she cried herself into a disturbed sleep.

My God that had hurt much more than she ever imagined.

She had maybe enjoyed the spanking a little, but not the rest of it.

Her dreamy thoughts turned to Adam. Would it be the same with him? Or would it be different when there was some sort of emotional attachment? When taking a punishment would be easier when you knew it would please your partner?

And would it be better when sex was involved after? Would that dull the pain?

So many questions. She now realised that these questions couldn't be answered by a session with Angela, no matter how authentic she made them.

Rachel had to play out her fantasy. With Adam. So she needed a plan.

She drifted off to sleep, still angry with Angela.

Next morning was dull and dreary. She moved around delicately. She touched her bum. But then made the mistake of lightly squeezing to feel the effect. The dull, painful ache told her all she wanted to know. She would be tender and bruised for days.

As she walked into the hallway, Rachel noticed a hand-written envelope in the pile. She recognised Angela's handwriting. Not ready to forgive her, she angrily threw it in the bin without opening it.

The other mail was a combination of junk mail and bills, plus a newsy postcard from an elderly relative.

Nothing exciting.

Rachel armed herself with a pen and paper. She knew, despite everything, that she wanted to see Adam again and that she would accept almost anything that went with it. So the pen and paper were to form a plan on how to contact him.

The easiest way was to contact him from his profile on the website. But that would need Angela's help

Then there was Google.

There couldn't be too many Adam De Veres who were successful businessmen, living somewhere in Surrey?

Maybe other similar sites would reveal something?

Maybe a chat with Alfonse at the restaurant! It suddenly hit her. Perhaps he would pass on a note to Adam? This had a definite chance of working! Adam had said he used the place about once a week, so the plan was definitely promising.

Rachel, from being down in the dumps from the pain and the crying, suddenly brightened.

She turned her attention to trying to forgive Angela. She fished the note out of her bin and read it.

Angela was upset. She had gone too far. Forgive her."

Hmmmm.

She mentioned that she did, on three separate occasions, offer Rachel an easy way out. That much was true.

Rachel had, on each occasion, chosen to continue with the severest route. That was her own fault, she supposed.

She had felt the need to be punished. Severely. And that is what she got. She didn't reckon she could hold it against Angela, who had warned her of the consequences all the way along the line.

OK, she would make up with her friend in a day or two, but she had decided there could be no more such episodes in future.

Rachel had discovered she was definitely submissive, but spankings without an emotional attachment were unsatisfying and simply not for her.

She was clear about what it was she wanted now

She was amazed at how far she had come in just a few short weeks.

Only a month or so ago, she hadn't given spanking much thought. Now she was desperate to offer herself and her bottom up to the charming stranger she had met by chance in a restaurant.

It felt weird.

It was weird.

But even as she sat gingerly on her well-whipped bottom, she knew then that she was going to do it, no matter what.

It was going to take a couple of weeks until the marks disappeared though, but there was no great rush. She guessed it wouldn't be a first date thing with Adam.

She looked forward to getting to know the object of her deepest fantasies better.

She smiled the smile of someone with a delicious secret.

Chapter Nine

Business is Business

Things were all in hand on Adam's Irish deal, but he had another business trip looming. This time to Amsterdam and he would need to be away for two to three weeks if he was to tie it all up.

His private aircraft had not completed the C check necessary to obtain the 'safe to fly' permission, so it would need to be a commercial flight again. Still, flights from Gatwick to Amsterdam were frequent and of a short duration. Most took less than an hour.

Business suits were all cleaned and his shirts impeccably laundered. Silk ties were carefully chosen. A couple of pairs of shoes were highly polished. He could easily pick up toiletries at the airport in Holland.

He was more than a little bored.

Occasionally he thought about Rachel and that lovely night in the restaurant. If only things had gone differently! Now he knew he was unlikely to see the gorgeous blonde again. She had created quite an impression on him. Ah well, he sighed.

He had registered himself on what he considered a more upmarket spanking site and had received a few responses.

One was from a quite attractive lady who lived fairly locally. He had decided to meet with her, over dinner. Adam arranged the rendezvous for a restaurant in Central London – not the same one where he met Rachel. They had a pleasant evening, but he soon decided she wasn't the one for him. She was a bit older, well-dressed end elegant. But she came over as a bit timid for his tastes. He couldn't imagine sensual, erotic encounters with a lady like that, so at the end of the evening he called her a cab and they parted.

He told her he would be in touch. He lied.

Adam definitely liked the girl next door type.

Dressy when the occasion called for it, but equally at home in jeans. Not too much make up, but just enough. Well cut hair. Nice perfume, but not too much.

He also liked blondes. He allowed the thought to cross his mind "Pretty much exactly like Rachel".

What a pity. Such a shame.

Adam Landed at Schiphol late morning on Tuesday. He walked to baggage reclaim, inwardly noting how spread out the airport was. It seemed like it was miles!

Having retrieved his bag, Adam passed customs and passport control and emerged from the airport to the taxi stand outside.

"Hoi. Het Waldorf Astoria alstublieft".

Adam spoke fluent Dutch and chatted easily with the taxi driver on the journey from the airport

As they pulled up outside the Astoria, one of the uniformed doormen opened the taxi door and smiled at Adam.

He was a regular at the hotel and all the staff knew and liked him. He was a good tipper too.

Adam had booked into the Backer Suite for this visit. There were bigger, more expensive suites, but they seemed overly extravagant for his purposes. The suite was still very expensive. It was elegant and contained everything he would need for hist visit.

Check in completed, he made a few phone calls about tomorrow's business and then stepped out into the bustle of central Amsterdam.

For this visit, he was a consultant to a Dutch company. He charged a large fee to advise them. Adam hadn't wanted to be directly involved in this deal. There were all sorts of complications when trying to asset strip a foreign company and he preferred not to be involved. Nevertheless, the fee he demanded was substantial and there was the prospect of future work too.

Adam strolled along to a decent bar and ordered a small beer. He knew Amsterdam well after many visits.

His mind idled.

He wondered if he'd find time to find a girl on De Wallen who might submit to his kinky desires. He had done this a few times before, but always came away with an empty feeling of dissatisfaction.

It was important to him to have an emotional attachment to the girls he saw. Someone who loved you so much that they willingly submitted to you, sensuously when they had done something to displease you. And still loved you afterwards.

All too often it was just a business transaction or the desire just to scratch the spanking itch and eventually these things became tiresome.

It took him by surprise how much Rachel popped into his mind and even fantasies. How he would love another chance to meet her.

At that moment, he made up his mind that when he returned, he would try to make contact with her.

He realised the ridiculousness of it all. For God's sake, she had turned him down; she didn't like the thought of a spanking. There was nothing positive he could say about the possibility of a relationship here.

But he knew he had to try.

He had to know.

Chapter Ten

Back in London

Rachel made her peace with Angela. After a couple of days, she texted her with "OK – I forgive you"

They arranged to go for a drink at the local pub that weekend. Sunday lunchtime.

To say Angela was relieved was a massive under-statement. She had never seen Rachel so tearful and angry.

Rachel and Angela hugged. They had never not spoken for more than a day or so, so this was a huge relief.

Rachel made it clear that anything like that was firmly in the past.

Angela agreed, after explaining that she had tried giving Rachel a get out three times, but Rachel had not opted out. She hadn't wanted to go that far, but Rachel seemed intent on taking things to the max. It seemed to Ange like she really wanted to find out, so she had continued.

Rachel told her she'd had a bit of difficulty walking home. That she'd sobbed for most of the night.

Angela felt awful.

Rachel saw this and tried to cheer her up.

"No lasting damage though. I can almost sit down now" she grinned ruefully.

"But you should see my bum! It's still got purple stripes a week later and the bruises are yellow, black, and purple. It's like an explosion in the proverbial paint factory!".

"I've never been in so much pain in all my life" she continued.

"But it's better now. I've had time to think."

Rachel explained her theory about the whole thing not meaning much without emotional attachment.

And explained her plan to meet with Adam again.

She even admitted that she needed to be spanked by him to find out once and for all what it was like. She told Angela that their little practice episode hadn't deterred her.

She knew now that she was submissive but needed to find out how it would be as part of a relationship".

"Good for you" said Angela "I admire you".

"Will you help me find him Ange?"

"Yes of course came the answer. And the friendship was back on track again.

"Rach" she added. "You do know that if you're going down that path, you're going to need to sleep with him sooner rather than later?"

"Yes" said Rachel. "And I'm damned well looking forward to it!"

They laughed out loud.

"So, what's your plan?" Ange asked.

"Multi-pronged actually" replied Rachel.

"Firstly, to get you to sort through your emails from him. That way I can get in tough my email.

"Ok, though I think all correspondence was via the sites messaging system. I'll take a look though. What's plan B?"

"Well, I could search for his profile on other sites and maybe find him that way? Or register myself, and see if he bites?"

"Oooh, not a good idea. Looking like you do, you will be inundated with replies – mostly from old perverts. There's a very real shortage of girls on these sites – a huge ratio of males to females. And girls as gorgeous as you? Very rare. I wouldn't waste your time if I were you."

"Hmm. OK, well how about plan C… to visit the restaurant I met Adam at and leave a note for him to call me? I think the waiter guy was called Alfonse. Adam told me he used the place once or twice a week?".

"Now THAT is a very good idea. Have you thought what you'd put in the note?"

"Just something light-hearted and funny – nothing desperate for sure," said Rachel.

"How about something like this – I have thought about you asking for my number and I'm afraid I lied to you – naughty me! I wanted to give it to you all along but didn't know how Angela would feel. So here it is. Please call me.'.

She would write her phone number underneath.

"Wow that's an extremely good one!", said Ange enthusiastically.

"That's almost bound to bring results if he's interested. And if he isn't he's, ever so slightly bonkers."

Rachel looked pleased. She'd write the note that evening and deliver it on Monday or Tuesday.

Exciting!

The lunchtime dragged on.

They happily chatted about anything and everything – even football.

The girls were well known in the pub. Normally two such beauties would have attracted lecherous glances in this male orientated pub, but that was long forgotten. They just somehow blended in now.

They decided not to bother to cook and so ordered two of the pub's famous Sunday roasts so they could continue chatting with each other.

Eventually, though, they would need to return home. There were clothes to prepare for the week. A bit of left-over housework was waiting for them too.

And there was a new detective series due to air on Sky.

And Rachel had an important note to write.

They reluctantly set off for home at about 4.30. A real shame as they were really enjoying each other's company.

Before they parted, Rachel asked Angela if she thought she should offer Alfonse a bit of a sweetener to make sure he delivered the note.

"No, it's not necessary in those sort of places" answered Angela. "They recognise a good customer when they see one".

They walked slowly back to their flats. Rachel was still a little stiff.

Once inside, Rachel dug out her writing paper and envelopes. "Who still had a writing set?", she asked herself.

She made herself a latte and set about writing the note for Adam

She screwed up and discarded two versions before she arrived at one which she thought would do nicely.

She had tried to write a note which would interest him enough to call.

She didn't know that she needn't have worried.

She had added 'I have revised my opinion on a subject which interests you and would like to talk to you about it, though I can't explain it at all well.'

Rachel sealed the scented envelope firmly and wrote "Mr Adam De Vere – Private and Confidential".

She carefully placed it in her bag. She would deliver it to Alfonse tomorrow evening.

And as a precaution, she checked that the restaurant was open on Monday evenings.

Thankfully, it was.

Chapter Eleven

In Amsterdam

Adam decided against going to De Wallen on that first evening. He was tired and he had important business the next day.

Instead, he opted for room service and a hotel Movie. But he dropped off whilst watching it.

He asked for a wake-up call at 6.30am – he had a bit of preparation still to do.

Carefully checking his clothes were immaculate, he retired properly for the night.

The wakeup call came what seemed like minutes afterwards.

He rose, showered, and shaved. He set about updating his meeting notes and then decided to skip breakfast.

He asked the reception desk to order him a car at 8.15. The company he was meeting was only about 2km away so that was plenty of time, even in the rush hour, to get there a little early.

The women of Amsterdam were undoubtedly pretty. He saw one who reminded him of Rachel for a moment.

"That bloody woman! I can't seem to get her off my mind!" he thought.

Still, it would have to wait a couple of weeks until he had tied up his business, he almost sighed. He was keen to get back in touch.

He'd even consider a relationship which didn't involve domination and submission, he conceded. She was lovely.

He didn't know that he had nothing to worry about.

So, the business of the day went smoothly. Adam shared many insightful things with the company which had employed him. He made acquisition look like a real, desirable possibility.

He had done some basic projections and the total value of the individual elements of the company far exceeded its trade.

He returned to the Astoria at about 4.30, having declined dinner that evening. He had decided to visit De Wallen after all that night, but he'd leave that until later.

A shower and a few beers came first.

At 6 o'clock he left the hotel and began wandering, fairly aimlessly, in the direction of the Red-Light district. Anything went if you had money in Amsterdam, and he had money.

He would have no problem hooking up with a girl who would allow spanking – severe spanking even – when the time came.

He ducked into the doorway of a bar he vaguely knew and ordered a small beer. This was turning out to be quite a relaxing trip.

He thought about later. What would it be tonight? He decided it should be a blonde, like Rachel. With a fabulous figure, like Rachel.

"Damn that girl" he said out loud. Whoever it was he hooked up with that night would be in for a good hard thrashing, he mused. Expensive but very much worth it to get rid of his frustration. And after that, he would bend her over and fuck her, hard and fast.

So, that was decided. How much would it cost him for one of the beautiful girls to endure that. €2,000 or €2,500 should probably cover it he reckoned.

He stopped in a couple more bars for more beer and final made his way into the neon signs lining the canal sides of De Wallen.

He walked into the first one he saw which looked a bit more upmarket, although all such establishments were clean and regulated.

The madame appeared. A lady in her early forties, elegantly dressed. She discreetly asked him what services he would like. And he told her.

"Ah, I'm afraid I don't have anyone who can help you here, but there is a place 50 yards down on this side who will be able to help. I will take you there and introduce you", she said helpfully.

They walked the fifty yards quickly and entered a rather flashier establishment.

The madame from the first place, quietly and discretely talked to the madame from the second, telling her what was required.

She returned to Adam.

"Yes, they have what you want, but I warn you, it will be expensive.

"For two hours with whoever you choose from that book, it will cost between €1,500 and €2,500. It all depends on who you pick."

"OK" said Adam, accepting the book. If you give me five minutes, I'll see if there is anything I want. One more thing, does that price include very hard caning?"

"One second". She went and talked again to the madame. She came back. "OK. Two hours with any girl in the book, €3000".

"Acceptable" said Adam. A few hundred Euros was nothing to him. And he had a lot of frustration to get rid of.

He looked through the pictures. The girls were all very pretty, but one in particular 'Heidi' was exactly what he was looking for. She even looked like Rachel and had a great figure. And what looked like the perfect bottom for a sound spanking.

Adam paid the €3,000 euros gladly.

Heidi was brought out for him. She was absolutely gorgeous.

"OK, said the madame. You have ten minutes out here, discussing what it is you want, then you go to a room. The two hours starts from when you go to the room, OK?"

"Yes, fine," said Adam.

Heidi spoke perfect English.

"I understand you want to spank and cane me. Very hard?" she said.

"Indeed. VERY hard. Is that going to be OK with you?".

She smiled. "Yes, it's fine. I won't be able to work for a day or so, which is why the price is what it is. But I have a very high pain threshold and I've been here before."

"And after that, I will probably want to fuck you very hard"

"Of course. What is your name please?"

Adam looked at the time. "From this moment on, my name is Sir. Now take me to the room. I'm going to enjoy this".

"Yes Sir" replied Heidi and with that she stood up, took his hand, and led him to a nice, surprisingly large and well-furnished backroom.

Heidi closed the door with a clunk and stood demurely in front of the closed door.

Adam inspected the room, which was obviously set up for clients with this sort of kink.

There was a large, sturdy desk, an armchair, and a bed with cushions.

In the corner was an umbrella stand full of canes, whips, and birches. On the coffee table were various paddles and heavy straps. Excellent.

He removed his jacket.

Heidi was well dressed. She wore a black, well-fitting cocktail dress and elegant flat shoes.

Adam sat on the armchair.

"Heidi" he barked "Come over to me now"

She obeyed

Adam looked her in the eye and told her that over the next two hours, she would be thoroughly punished. And it started right now.

He made her take her shoes off and told her to bend over his knee. She did so immediately. Something in Adam's voice told her he meant business.

She placed herself over Adam's knee and waited.

"I am now going to spank you for thirty minutes. Please cry and scream as much as you want, because no one will come and help you" he warned

She felt her fitted skirt being unfastened and helpful shuffled her bottom up so he could take it off.

She then raised her bottom again as he slipped her knickers – her lovely black silk briefs – down to her ankles.

He looked down and saw the gorgeous unblemished bottom and then he began,

Slowly at first. A blow on each cheek alternately. The spanking got continually harder. The blows became less spaced out. He occasionally became tired and took a break,

Heidi was taking the hard spanking very well, just the occasional squeal.

As it went on, Heidi's bottom became first bright red, then more of a purple shade.

Five minutes to go. It was hurting now, but she knew there was much worse to come. She didn't make a fuss.

Adam spanked her furiously for most of the rest of the time. Fast, hard, forceful. Heidi's legs kicked out in all directions but still she didn't make a sound. Adam was impressed.

At last Adam had delivered his last spank. The half hour was up.

Heidi was sent to the corner whilst Adam decided what to do next.

He walked up to her in the corner and gently kissed her neck as she faced the wall.

He ran his hands freely over Heidi's shapely bum, squeezing occasionally as she groaned.

He felt her wetness with his probing fingers. Now she was groaning in pleasure.

All the time he was thinking about what was coming next.

He left her in the corner and walked to the chunky desk. This would do fine, he thought.

He pulled it out a little. He thought about placing cushions on it but decided it was a bit silly, considering the pain he was about to inflict.

"Come here Heidi" he ordered.

She walked over to him, naked form the waist down.

"Now remove the rest of your clothes". She stood in front of him.

Again, Heide obliged immediately. She stood completely naked in front of him

"Listen very carefully." He said, holding her chin firmly in his hand, forcing her to face him.

"I now intend to whip your bottom very hard, thirty times at least. In between batches of ten, I will apply the paddle and the strap, 30 times each. It may cause grazes and it will be extremely painful."

"Yes Sir". Heide gulped.

Adam selected a long-handled leather riding crop, about as thick as a pencil and all of two feet in length.

He swooshed it, satisfyingly, through the air.

"Now, bend over my desk..... no, right over so you are on tiptoe".

Heidi knew that the best position was with legs slight apart, and automatically assumed position.

Adam measured the crop across her red and purple bottom. He lifted the whip right back, high above his shoulder.

Heidi knew that she would truly earn her money in this next hour.

The crop landed with a huge 'CRAAACKK!' Right across the seat of her bum. About a second after landing, the searing pain of a hard stroke zipped through her body. Her feet left the floor, she couldn't help but squeal.

It made no difference to Adam. He continued with the whipping, every stroke at full force until he reached ten. Heidi was now sobbing heavily.

Adam was unmoved. He picked up the leather paddle and proceeded to cover her whole bottom with 30 paddle trokes as hard as he had ever given, after which he allowed Heidi a short rest. He allowed her to rub her bottom.

But all too soon, for Heidi at least, he resumed with the crop, picking up where he left off.

Adam thrashed her 10 more times in quick succession. It was agony for Heidi who tried to jump up once. But Adam pushed her back down into position and she got an extra two strokes.

He went and picked up the thick leather strap. Heidi groaned. She usually took punishment well but was finding it hard with this one.

Adam laid the strap across her bottom and administered first 15 strokes to one side of her bottom and then 15 to the other.

Heidi bawled her eyes out.

Adam again allowed her a small respite so she could ease the deep ache in her bum by rubbing it.

Then it was back into position to finish the beating.

"Please Sir?"

"Shut up Heidi. If you're not back over that desk immediately you will get six extras".

Heidi almost dived over the desk in a desire not to merit extra punishment,

Adam resumed the whipping, this time taking a step up before delivering each stroke very deliberately

Somehow, amazingly, Heidi managed to keep in position, blubbing quietly as each searing stroke was delivered.

When the 30th stroke landed Adam looked at his watch. Good. Twenty minutes of the session were left.

He looked at Heidi's bottom, which was a mass of purple welts and bruises. There were even a few places where the skin had been broken. She had earned her money! Adam didn't like to break the skin, but sometimes it happened. He would apply some cream in a minute.

So he walked behind her. Her tear-stained face looked anxiously over her shoulder.

She needn't have worried. Adam was unzipping his trousers. He discarded them and his boxers too. She was relieved.

Adam closed up behind her. She winced. Checking with his finger to see if she was still dripping wet - amazingly she was.

He parted her thighs and thrust his rock-hard penis straight into her. He held onto her shoulders and continued to furiously slam it all the way in and most of the way out. His hips caused her massive discomfort as he slammed them against her bottom, hard and fast.

In a few short seconds he came, but Heidi was absolutely amazed that she did too. A long, breath-taking orgasm. She had never come close to orgasm with a client before that night – and there had been many hundreds of them. Far too many for her to count, she thought.

Adam made sure Heidi was OK. He then dressed and left the room, leaving a good tip for Heidi

He put on his jacket and walked out into the night air.

They had both learned something from that session.

Heidi learned that intense punishment gave her intense, back arching orgasms.

Adam had learned that almost gently spanking a loved one was far, far better than really thrashing someone irrelevant.

He felt less frustrated now, but still a little bit empty.

Again, he realised that punishments didn't really add up to much, unless they were submitted to lovingly. The person being punished had to want to be corrected to please him, and not simply do it for money.

Enlightening.

Depressing.

Chapter Twelve

Time for the Plan

Rachel had few appointments on the Monday. It was traditionally mostly phone enquiries on a Monday. People who had been looking over the weekend.

She dealt with them politely and easily.

She was, all the time, worrying about her note. Worrying if Adam would laugh at its content. Could she go through with it?

5.30 came after the day had dragged. She would go to Chelsea by bus as cabs were expensive,

She applied a little make up, brushed her hair, and jumped onto the bus, checking the note was still in her bag.

The bus took quite a while in the rush hour traffic of central London. She changed buses and didn't arrive in Chelsea until after seven o'clock.

Rachel walked down the street to the restaurant. Damn! It was closed! She read the opening hours sign and saw it opened at 7:30 on a Monday

She looked at her watch – it was 7.10 so she didn't have too long to wait. She decided to go to a pub a few doors away.

On entering, she found herself in a nice, very trendy bar – all chrome and glass.

She ordered and gin and tonic and sat down in the nearest thing she could find to a quiet corner to complete her worrying.

Could she do this?

Time ticked by and soon she had finished her drink. It was half past.

She made her way back to the now open restaurant. There was no sign of Alfonse. She was very nervous as she asked the man who greeted her "Hi. I'm not actually dining tonight, but may I speak to Alfonse please?".

"Ah. Alfonse doesn't start until eight-thirty tonight I'm afraid. Can I help?"

"Umm" this had thrown her. "No thank you, I do need to see him briefly, but I can come back after 8:30. I have plenty I can be doing in the meantime" she lied.

And so Rachel found herself back in the rather pleasant chrome and glass bar, sipping another G & T.

Another 45 minutes to worry about the ridiculousness of all this, she thought to herself. What would a confident, charming, rich businessman who probably had his pick of female company, think?

Well, fortified by a couple of Gins, she was bloody well going to have a try, having come this far.

She returned to the restaurant at 8:35 and was relieved to be greeted by Alfonse.

"Good evening Madam" he smiled politely, not quite remembering where he had seen her before. But Rachel had made a big enough impression for him to know that he had most certainly seen here before.

"Good evening Alfonse". She started confidently.

"I was here a while ago with Mr Adam De Vere she explained.

Ah! That was it! The lovely blonde caught in the rain!

Rachel continued. "I was wondering if you had seen him recently. I have some news for him" again she lied.

"Mr De Vere was here, now let me see, four days ago, but I'm afraid he's out of the country on business for a couple of weeks.

"OK" said a crest-fallen Rachel, fishing the note out of her handbag. "Would you mind giving him this note on his return, please?"

"Certainly madam" smiled Alfonse reassuringly, "I will make sure personally that he gets it as soon as he next visits us, please rest assured".

Rachel thanked him and with that, she left to return to the suburbs. It had been a bit nerve-wracking, but it was over now.

She felt light-headed and so she returned to the bar and ordered herself one more Gin to 'celebrate'.

Someone had sat in 'her' seat now, so she sat on a stool at the bar.

One young man tried his luck with the gorgeous blonde sitting at the bar.

"Good evening. Could I buy you a drink?" he smiled, politely.

Rachel smiled back.

"I'm sorry, but I'm just about to leave. And I have a boyfriend." Yet again she lied. This was becoming a habit.

A bad one.

Rachel drained her glass and left.

It was nice to feel appreciated though.

On the bus home, she texted Ange.

'Well, I've done it! The plan is in motion! The note has been delivered to Alfonse but Adam's out of the country for two weeks. Bugger! Just my luck, eh? I'll just have to be patient then'

Angela replied within a few minutes.

'Language! LOL. I'm excited for you. Hope it all goes as you hope xx'

So do I. So do I, Rachel muttered under her breath.

Because it's going to be fantastic if it does.

She arrived home and got ready for bed. The G & T's had made her a bit woozy.

Once again, she undressed in front of the wardrobe mirror, imagining Adam was enjoying looking at her.

Rachel was pleased with what she saw.

He was in for the ride of his life, she vowed as her face pressed on the mirror. She closed her eyes masturbated furiously at these thoughts, pressed up against the cold glass.

It didn't take long at all. She arched her back in a breath-taking orgasm as she reached her climax. She remained perfectly still as the waves subsided, anxious to feel every single sensation.

She felt like she'd never had an orgasm as good as that before.

She hadn't.

Chapter Thirteen

Now the Waiting

Two weeks was going to seem like forever!

Rachel hung out with Ange a few times – going for a drink and to the cinema.

But everything she tried wasn't much of a distraction.

She was nervous about exactly what she would say to Adam, but she was determined to see it through.

She could truthfully say she really enjoyed their dinner together and truthfully say she regretted no giving him her phone number.

That the fact that he was going to meet Ange for spanking sessions had completely thrown a spanner in the works. She hadn't ever considered an opinion on this subject, let alone considered starting some sort of relationship with a man who clearly enjoyed it.

That they would have to take things slowly. That she had confided in a friend that she wished to know Adam better but there was a possible problem with his 'tastes'.

That it turned out her friend had some experience in these matters and offered to show her what it felt like

That she had accepted a spanking from him out of curiosity. Nothing too hard and mostly clothed.

That she found being spanked exciting – she hadn't actually *enjoyed* the spanking, but the moments before and the memory after were huge turn-ons.

Maybe she wouldn't mention that the friend was called Angela!

That maybe they could see each other for a while to see where this took them – dinners out, maybe the odd weekend away, maybe just drinks.

Rachel knew this would inevitably lead to her sleeping with Adam. And she was excited by the idea.

She also knew that, after a while – maybe a few weeks – this would lead to her being spanked.

She wondered how it would be. If it would be loving or punishing.

She decided it didn't matter which. Either way was OK by her. Hear head was completely in the game and she would submit to anything with her fantasy man now.

Rachel was concerned that she was becoming obsessed with Adam. What if he didn't WANT a relationship of any sort? In a month or two, he had come to mean a lot to her. They had only met once for goodness sake. It was hard to believe that she felt this strongly; cared this deeply; was prepared to be submit to anything by this man.

He was a virtual stranger.

But in her heart, she knew this was meant to be.

The days dragged by until Adam's return. Rachel had no idea that their thoughts had been running in parallel. That he would be trying to contact her when he got back.

But nothing. No call, no text. She was about to give up on him when, one Friday evening, a text arrived! It was from Adam.

'Hi Rachel. May I call you tomorrow evening? I was very pleased to receive your note - we have a huge amount to discuss."

Rachel was thrilled. She had butterflies in her tummy.

How should she reply?

After a few minutes thought, she replied 'Yes. That would be very nice.' And then, as a naughty afterthought she added to it before sending.

"Yes. That would be very nice. Sir".

She wanted him to be in no doubt who would be in charge if they formed this relationship.

'Wow! Now that IS a pleasant surprise. Let's talk'.

'Yes let's' was all she could think of to say as they agreed that Adam should phone her at 6pm next day.

She would have a few glasses of wine with Angela before the call.

Get some advice on how to play it for the important call.

It was vital she didn't throw herself at Adam, she knew that much.

She texted Ange and they arranged lunch at the local pub. It was a Saturday, but they still offered a good selection of meals and bar food.

She couldn't sleep for excitement, despite a luxuriant bath and a warm drink before bed.

This was just too exciting.

Chapter Fourteen

Saturday

Rachel awoke from a fitful sleep of twisted dreams.

It took her a while to realise she was, indeed, awake.

She looked at her alarm and it was after nine. She was never still in bed after nine! She shot out of bed and through the shower.

Now filly refreshed and awake, she turned her thoughts to the day ahead. Lunch with her friend, followed by a very important phone call which might change the rest of her life.

The butterflies came back.

Rachel pulled on her tight jeans and a clean polo top.

She had arranged to meet Ange at 12:30 and so she found herself with a couple of hours to fill.

So she nipped to the supermarket and did her weekly shopping before lunch.

She walked into the pub a minute or two late.

Angela was already there and waved cheerily.

Rachel joined her at the quiet table she had thoughtfully chosen. She got a round of drinks in and sat down with her friend.

"Tell me all about it then" said Ange, eagerly.

"Nothing to tell yet" answered Rachel

"You can look at the texts we swapped" and she handed her phone to her friend.

Ange read the texts.

"Wow!" she remarked. "Sir, eh? You aren't messing about are you? Making your intentions crystal clear!".

"If that doesn't intrigue him, then I'd give up!"

Rachel blushed slightly.

"Well, no point in beating about the bush" and then said "did that sound very wrong? I didn't mean it to!"

They both collapsed into a fit of giggles.

They asked for menus and ordered a light lunch, accompanied by a cheap and cheerful bottle of Sauvignon Blanc.

Rachel had to keep her wits about her for the call, later.

They chatted about how the phone call might go.

They started on a list for Rachel of the things she really wanted to say.

How she had been thinking about their lovely dinner a lot

How she had wished she'd handed over her number so she could get to know him more.

The need to go slowly – perhaps a few dinner dates if he would like?

Leading to a weekend away maybe?

Leading to who knows what?

She needed to tell her about normal, everyday things and the call needed to be easy. Natural.

Her job, whereabouts she lived, what she liked to do in any spare time she had.

And it mustn't be all about her. Apart from spanking (Ha!), what did Adam enjoy?

They drew up the list, crossed one or two out. Added a few more in.

They copied the revised list out again to come up with the final draft

Rachel read it back, out loud.

Ange approved. She suggested that, once they were talking easily, Rach told Adam that she had made a list of the things she wanted to say and read it to him. That way she wouldn't miss anything out because Adam had interrupted her train of thought by talking and Rachel thought this was a good plan.

She would have a check list to make certain she expressed herself exactly as she meant to.

Lunch finished, wine emptied, it was now four o'clock.

They slowly walked back to their flats and said their goodbyes.

Angela wished Rachel all the luck in the world.

She knew that this was really important to her friend, and she wanted Rachel's plan to succeed.

Rachel sat down to wait for Adam's call.

What if he didn't ring? She started to feel nervous.

Only an hour to go now.

She had decided she was going to take the call in her bedroom, where she could relax.

She carefully placed the script she had made and a bottle of chilled vodka on the bedside table.

All sorts of thoughts went through her mind. 6 o'clock came and went.

He's not going to call, thought Rachel, dejectedly.

But just after five past, the phone rang.

She jumped with a start. Butterflies in the tummy again.

It was Adam!...

Chapter Fifteen

The Call

"Rachel speaking".

Blast it! She had answered the phone very formally in her nervousness.

"Hi Rachel. Lovely to talk to you again". Said Adam.

"Firstly let me say how delighted I was to receive tour note from Alfonse" he said.

"If you knew how much I had been thinking about the beautiful blonde lady I met by chance, you wouldn't be nervous" he went on.

"Is it too much to hope for that the feeling might have been mutual?".

"No. I've been thinking about you an awful lot too. I have SO many questions, SO many embarrassing things to admit" said Rachel.

"But I would very much like it if we could see each other again."

"That's brilliant. I've just come back from Amsterdam on business. I only got your note a few days ago. And since then I've been wondering exactly what to say to you!"

"Dinner tomorrow?", he invited?

"Lovely." She replied.

"But let's talk a bit more now, please"

"Absolutely"

Adam decided to take the bull by the horns.

"OK, well, you already know that I have some, shall we say, unusual pre-delictions from your friend?"

"Yes". She blushed.

"I know this is embarrassing, but what do you think of that?" he went on.

"Well, at first I thought it was very strange – a handsome man resorting to meeting online. "And for those purposes! I was convinced Angela had had a lucky escape from a pervert!" she laughed. He joined in.

"That's why I didn't give you my number" she revealed.

"And is that what you still feel?", he asked.

"No" said Rachel emphatically.

"I told you that I confided in a friend that I had met an attractive businessman, extremely eligible. I also told him of your 'hobbies'. Turned out he was experienced in these areas, and he offered me some appreciation lessons! And it turned out, although I'd never even thought about it before you, I actually liked the feeling and excitement of a spanking. And I reckon, after being particularly bad, a caning might do me good, not that I'd look forward to it...." She tailed off her outpouring.

"Wow. Excellent." said Adam.

"But, if we get on, this is something we will naturally progress to. Not straight away – we'll need to feel our way slowly. Would that be OK Adam?"

"Absolutely Rachel" he replied.

She took a large swig from the vodka bottle! The ice had been broken.

"So what do you like to get up to?" Adam asked.

"Oooh I guess it's normal sorts of things. Theatre, eating out, foreign travel" she replied.

"Although I haven't been anywhere much. In fact I haven't been away at all for the last three years. Where does the time go?.

"I know" he empathised.

"What places have you been to then?"

"The usual touristy ones. Spain, Italy, Greece, Turkey. I absolutely love the Aegean Coast of Turkey – have you ever been to Didim / Altinkum? It's busy but there are some very beautiful places there".

"Never been, but I understand it's really lovely around there. With a good party to boot!" he replied.

They chatted in an increasingly comfortable way, laughing as they shared experiences.

Time flew. It was nearly eight o'clock when Rachel remembered her list.

She took another swig from the vodka bottle.

"Oh! I forgot to read this out!" she said. "It's a list of all the things I'd decided I wanted to say to you!"

"Fire away then"

"Hang on".

Rachel quickly reviewed the list but decided that everything on it had been covered naturally.

Even the spankings. It seemed so normal.

"Well How about Tuesday for Dinner?"

"That would be great, thank you" said Rachel.

"Shall I book a table at the same place as last time? Eight o'clock OK?" asked Adam

"Lovely. I'll wear something more appropriate than Jeans this time!".

He laughed. "You looked great to me", he said chivalrously.

"One last thing.." he said before putting the phone down.

"Yes?"

"You only need to call me 'Sir' when you've been bad!."

"OK, Sir" she flirted, cheekily.

They put their phones down.

That couldn't have gone better thought Rachel.

And it couldn't.

Chapter Sixteen

Angela's secret

Ever since her 'practice' session with Rachel, Angela had discovered something.

She had enjoyed the feeling of power when she punished Rachel. She had enjoyed Rachel's discomfort, she was ashamed to admit to herself.

She had enjoyed the moments when she took her knickers off; felt the weight of her beautiful body over her lap.

Bouncing her hand repeatedly on her friends bum while Rachel wriggled helplessly.

She had enjoyed seeing those cane marks appearing on the unblemished bottom.

She decided she would like to try this dominant role again.

So Angela set about changing her profile on the spanking website.

"Beautiful 28-year-old Dominant from London." She started and followed it with the details.

She used keywords like spanking, CP, moderate to severe and more

She filled in the profile stating she was looking for males or females around her own age.

She said that she did not charge a fee, which seemed unusual on that site

She invited replies form the London area.

She said she would accommodate or travel.

Ange developed an attractive profile, pitched to result in a number of responses so she could choose someone suitable from them.

She pixelated her face on a photo of her in a leather mini skirt, loaded it to the profile. It showed off her great figure and posted the profile for approval.

Surely that would attract a few responses, she thought.

She had a surprise coming.

When she checked her mailbox next morning, she had had over a hundred replies!

She began to work through them, one by one.

Too old

Too far away

Sounds like a pervert

Married

Wanting a 'Mummy'

Unattractive photo

For every twenty replies, she had worked it down to around one possible

There were six or seven possible. She was excited. It included two women who didn't want Lesbian sex.

She put the possibles aside to return to later.

By the time she did so, another fifty responses had come in!

Ange now had ten good prospects – she had included six more but had excluded a few after a second read.

Of these, two were from females and the rest from males.

Ange thought about this a lot. She would probably be safer if she met girls to start with…. And she had enjoyed the session with Rachel.

She carefully read the replies and the profiles of the two girls. Both had pictures. But one was particularly attractive and fairly local.

She decided to try to build a 'relationship' with that one – a girl called Jane, so she set about writing back to her.

Jane seemed pretty much ideal. She was thirty, lived 40 minutes away. Far enough! Liked to be spanked hard. Was not an out-

and-out lesbian. They had interests in common. She looked good.

'This could be exciting!', thought Ange.

She replied, thanking Jane for responding. Asking if she had any questions. Jane admitted she had had just a little experience but was absolutely positive that she would be moving this forward through a meeting or a series of meetings with suitable girls.

Over the next week or two, the two swapped details and chatter.

They decided that a phone call would be the best way forward and when they chatted, they seemed to get on well.

They arranged to meet for a coffee.

Ange was stunned at how good-looking Jane was when they met. She was a shy girl, which made talking about what they were planning difficult at first, but she got over this.

They set some ground rules and then Ange invited Jane over to her place for dinner the following week.

Making it plain that Jane would be getting more than dinner.

A lot more.

Chapter Seventeen

Back at the restaurant

It was Tuesday already and Rachel was excited! She had been shopping and bought a lovely little black dress and beautiful grey shoes.

She had visited the hairdresser for a few highlights in her hair.

She had a manicure and her finger and toenails painted beautifully.

She had bought new, expensive lingerie

It was the very best she could look. And she looked truly stunning.

She couldn't afford it really, but this somehow seemed worth it.

She had talked each day with Adam, and they seemed at ease with each other.

Adam told her that he had reserved a special 'quiet' table at the restaurant. One where, if they wanted, they could talk about anything without being overheard.

Rachel shivered. She knew exactly what he meant.

"Good" she found herself saying.

She had decided to take a cab all the way to the restaurant. Sod the expense.

She finished applying her make up just as the cab arrived at her flat. She had been keeping an eye out for it. With one last look in the mirror, she went downstairs and got into the cab, directing the driver to the eatery.

"You look nice love", remarked the cabbie. "Someone special?".

Rachel smiled but didn't answer. It was none of his business.

Instead, she changed the subject. She didn't want to be rude.

"Lovely evening" she said.

They chatted every now and then during the journey. But nothing too personal. The cabbie had got the message it seemed.

By the time the taxi pulled up outside the restaurant, it was a minute or two after eight. The taxi was paid off and Rachel inspected herself in the window before she went in.

Alfonse greeted her like an old friend.

"Good evening" he smiled.

"Evening Alfonse" Rachel replied, also smiling widely.

Alfonse took her to the table Adam had reserved. He rose from his seat and kissed her.

Defying convention, he kissed her lightly. On the lips

"Wow!" was all he could say.

So elegant, So classy. So sexy.

"Will I do?", asked Rachel

"You look absolutely beautiful, Rachel. I am privileged to be having dinner with the best-looking lady in the restaurant. No. Not the restaurant. In London."

She blushed a little but was pleased.

Alfonse pulled out her seat for her to sit.

He presented the couple, for that is what they were becoming, with the dinner menus. He explained the 'specials of the day' and left them to choose. Alfonse knew when to be attentive and when not.

When he returned they had both chosen starters of carpaccio and then mains of Guinea Fowl stuffed with apricots and pine nuts – a North African feel this evening.

They started talking about anything and everything, laughing a great deal. This was compatibility gone mad!

A little bit of Dutch courage and Rachel was brave enough to broach the elephant in the room.

"Adam", she asked quietly. "I want to know more about your little kink. Spanking girls like me. Do you mind?"

"No, not at all. You can ask me anything", he answered. "What is it you want to know?"

"Well", she started nervously, "lots of things really. Do you enjoy really hurting? Or is it erotic?".

"OK – well the truthful answer is both", said Adam. "There are times I want eroticism that spanking gives me. There are also times when it feels very sexy for me to punish partners more severely. When they have behaved very badly for example"

"Thank you" Rachel replied. "And who decides what is bad behaviour and what is flirtatious naughtiness, if I can put it that way?"

"Oh that's easy. Me!" he laughed

"So I have no say in it?"

"I'm trying to be absolutely honest here" said Adam. "The truthful answer to that is none when in a relationship with me. I know it's chauvinistic. I know it's selfish. But that is how it has to be with me".

He then added quickly "ARE we in a relationship? It feels very much like that to me", he said, leaning across the table to kiss her properly, passionately. It was perhaps a good job he had picked a table out of the line of sight of the other diners.

Rachel's heart did a flip. "Absolutely. Definitely." She answered breathlessly.

Adam leant back an explained some more.

"When I am with someone, then we need to discuss a way of behaving very early on. A set of ground rules if you like. And transgressions have consequences. Sometimes very painful consequences. And I realise this is all one-sided, but again, that's how it is. If you can't accept this, then I'm afraid we're just not going to make it, beautiful though you are".

"Oh Adam!" said Rachel staring directly into Adams soft brown eyes. "I'd do anything to be with you. I know that already. And I have even tried out the pain with a friend, as I told you. I have to admit it excited me."

"Go on" said Adam

"I'm looking forward to this type of relationship. I will try to please you and if I don't you will make sure – through hard spankings, whippings, and canings – that I know I have displeased you. And I will endeavour to be better.

But not TOTALLY better!". She laughed.

"Good" said Adam, pleased.

"What about if I'm just a little cheeky? Or I flirt with someone say?".

"That's easy" smiled Adam. "I'll assume you are doing it because you want a spanking. Which I will, at the next appropriate opportunity, happily administer."

"Thank you" Rachel replied. "One more question please?"

He nodded.

"What is your favourite implement to deal with the naughtiest girls?"

"Easy", responded Adam. "Far and away it's the cane. And if you're going to ask me why, I'll tell you. Because it hurts when I want it to hurt. Really badly. Because it makes little noise."

"Thank you, Sir" said Rachel.

"Don't mention it" Adam replied. "Anything else?"

"No Sir!" Rachel found herself saying quietly.

There was no doubt she had been thoroughly turned on by Adam's answers.

"Well there is one more thing, yes" she said.

"What is it?"

"When can we get together to agree the ground rules for all this?", Rachel asked. "Because it really can't come soon enough for me"

She was amazed by just how bold she was being.

"Well, why don't you come over to mine for the weekend next week?", he said. "I'm away on business this coming weekend, but I'm totally free the week after. I'm not presuming anything.", he added hastily. "Separate bedrooms of course."

Rachel looked deep into those brown eyes again.

She knew they were growing very close to their relationship moving on and she welcomed it.

She knew then that separate bedrooms would not be required.

Not next weekend or ever.

Chapter Eighteen

Angela plays out her secret

So, Angela was busy preparing for her meet with Jane.

She had checked and Jane had no special dietary requirements, and so she decided on lasagne with green beans and tomato for the mains. That wouldn't take too much looking after – pretty much oven to table.

She did a retro prawn cocktail as starters. Easy again – fridge to table.

There was a shop bought gateau for dessert and, if Jane was still hungry after that lot, she had some cheese and biscuits handy in the tin. That should do fine.

She decided to deal with Jane before dinner.

Now, what should she wear?

Ange went to her wardrobe. She picked out a smart navy business suit. Tight fitting. She would need to take the jacket off when it came to the spanking.

She hadn't told Jane what to wear and wondered what she would choose for the occasion.

Ange was looking forward to this evening very much.

Now she sat down to think it all through. She had decided that tonight's punishment would be a hand spanking and maybe the hairbrush, unless it became clear Jane needed more.

Hmm. Ange put the can in the sideboard, just in case it was required, but she didn't think it would be. Jane had seemed quite timid when they met for coffee.

Time flew by and before she knew it, it was time to get ready.

Ange showered and fixed her hair. She went for the severe, scraped back look. She applied hake up and carefully dressed.

She readied music on the media player – just in case the neighbours overheard!.

Finally, she was ready. And excited.

They had arranged for Jane to call at 7:30 and the doorbell duly rang at just before that time.

Good. She was punctual.

"Hi", greeted Ange, unsure how to greet her guest. Or was it victim? In the end she just went for a quick hug and a kiss on the cheek.

Jane was obviously nervous. "Shall I call you Miss?" she asked timidly.

"Not yet. Let's go I the kitchen and have a glass of wine. Then I can tell you what this evening will bring!".

The walked through to the kitchen. Ange poured them both a glass of white wine and turned on a little background music.

"Have you been nervous about being spanked" asked Ange, casually.

"Yes, a bit" replied Jane. "But I was determined to go through with it. We got on so well when we had coffee, I thought". It was more of a question.

"Yes, I thought it was really exciting too", replied Ange.

Draining their wine glasses, Angela spoke.

"Want to know what happens next?"

"In a minute or two, we'll go next door. I will shut the curtains. From that point on, you will call me Miss. Understand?" she said gently.

"Yes Miss" said Jane, looking at the floor.

"I will ask you about any recent misbehaviour. And don't think of saying you have done nothing wrong! That merits a punishment on its own!"

"I will send you to the corner while I consider an appropriate punishment, then call you back over to me. You will with either agree, in which place I will carry it out there and then, or else you disagree, in which case you will leave immediately. Am I making myself plain?"

"Absolutely Miss"

"Look at me when you are talking to me!"

Jane snapped her head up and made eye contact.

Providing you accept your punishment, I will leave you alone for a few minutes to pull yourself together, then you will be called to join me in the kitchen. We can drink more wine and then have dinner. Does that sound OK?"

"Perfectly, Miss. It's pretty much what I was imagining."

Ange took Jane's arm and said, "Now go through to the lounge and wait for me."

Jane obeyed.

As Angela watched her walk through to the lounge, she noticed that Jane was wearing a short, loose skirt. She wore a little make up and a tight blouse. Perfect, she thought, watching her bottom jiggle as she walked. This was going to be fun.

Now, Jane. Tell me about any recent bad behaviour please. Lateness, Swearing, Laziness – you know the sort of thing I mean".

"Well said Jane thoughtfully "I've been late for work twice this week for a start" she admitted. "Also, there's this guy at work. He really likes me. I've flirted with him, but I have no interest in him".

"Right", said Ange. "That's enough to be going on with, I think. "Go to the corner and stand with your face to the wall Jane!" she said sternly.

She went out to the kitchen and poured herself a sneaky glass of wine. She drank it and went back to the Lounge.

Ange walked slowly and deliberately up to Jane's corner. Jane could feel the hot breath close to her ear as she was told, very strictly, what would happen next.

"In a moment, I'm going to go and sit down on the sofa. When I tell you, you will come to me and stand on my right side. I will take you over my knee and spank you, very hard, for five minutes at my own speed".

"Yes miss"

"I will then lift your skirt and repeat the dose for another 5 minutes, after which you will stand up and I will take you pants down and administer another 10 minutes. All at my own pace. Understood?"

"Yes Miss"

"I will then pick up my ebony hairbrush and continue to beat your bottom for as long as I see fit. During the punishment, I may rub your bottom. Don't be surprised by this"

"It will be very painful, I hope you understand that. After the punishment, I will apply cream to reduce any bruising."

"Now – is that clear?"

"Yes Miss".

"And do you accept the punishment is deserved and fair?"

"(Gulp) Yes Miss".

Angie went and sat on the middle cushion of the sofa, hanging her jacket on a dining chair as she went.

She sat and then said, "Come here now!"

Jane almost ran to her side, looking flushed.

"Right" said Angela. "Now you know why you are here, so bend over my knee immediately". She was enjoying this!

Jane obeyed. She didn't dare do otherwise.

Ange felt powerful and in control as the beautiful Jane laid over her lap, awaiting her punishment.

Jane screwed her eyes tight shut as the punishment started. Ange started lightly, placing smacks all over Jane's bottom and thighs.

After five minutes, Jane felt her skirt being folded up and over her back

Ange delighted at the delicate underwear. And then proceeded to administer punishment – a little harder this time – to the already reddening bottom. It was still not particularly hard. But it was getting there!

And after the second five minutes, Angela slowly slipped her thumbs into the sides of Jane's pants. Slowly, slowly she tugged at them until they slid down to her knees. Wonderful.

She inspected the damage so far – just a red all over bottom so far. She thought Jane would be expecting a bit more.

She laid her hand on Jane's bottom and felt the heat.

"Now it's time to get serious" she said, setting about her work with gusto.

She worked really hard at punishing the bare bottom and thighs on her lap. Sometimes slaps on alternate cheeks, sometimes spaced out between hard smacks, sometimes a series on spanks in quick succession.

Jane was taking her punishment well, but Angela had worked up to a very hard spanking by now. She couldn't help but let out the occasional sob or squeal. But Ange continued regardless.

After 10 further minutes, Jane was crying. Not moaning about the punishment. It was, in fact a huge turn on. But it hurt.

Angela rubbed Jane's bottom to relieve the pain. Jane moaned. Was it pleasure? She continued anyhow.

Respite given, Ange picked up the ebony hairbrush. She brought it down with a real Thwack! On Jane's poor bottom. Hard and in quick succession. Covering the whole are thoroughly.

When she judged Jane had had enough, she put down the brush.

"Good." Said Ange. "You took that very well.

"Now get dressed and go and stand back in the corner."

"Thank you, Miss" said Jane, quietly

She went out to the kitchen to check Dinner was on course. It was.

Back in the lounge, she released Jane from her corner time and handed her a glass of chilled wine.

"It's Ange now" she said softly.

"And wash your face in the bathroom and I'll serve dinner. You OK?"

"Oh yes definitely. I've been needing that for a while".

They enjoyed their dinner and chatted freely now. Jane came out of her shell and admitted it had been a huge turn on. She was with a guy who didn't enjoy spanking her, but she really needed it. He had no clue that Jane had come to see Ange. She could now go home and think all about it while they were in bed.

Hmm. "Lucky her" thought Ange.

They decided they should meet regularly, maybe once a month, so Angela could make sure Jane was behaving,

Somehow, she knew that she wouldn't be.

Chapter Nineteen

Eventually it's weekend

Rachel was at a bit of a loss for what to do until that weekend came.

Angela wasn't available quite so much it seemed, although they did go to the pub on the Saturday.

Rachel told her all about how things had moved along.

Ange couldn't bring herself to tell Rachel her delicious secret.

Both were happy.

Of course, Adam rang Rachel every day or so. He arranged to send his driver to pick her up and take her to his place on the Friday after work.

She objected at first, but realised she wouldn't have a clue how to find the place and so she gave in.

What would they make of a chauffeur driven top-of-the range Bentley in the semis of suburban Hillingdon!

"Oh and Rachel?" he added at the end of one such call. "I like white undies". And he put the phone down!

The cheek of the man. He was presuming an awful lot for what was only their third or fourth meeting! But, she sighed happily, he was right to presume.

After an eternity, the waiting came to an end. It was Friday. It was 6 pm and Rachel looked anxiously out of the curtains.

The Bentley pulled up right on time. Rachel was certain a few curtains twitched as the driver donned his cap, put on his hazard lights, and sent Rachel a text.

'I hope I'm outside' it said.

'Out in a jiffy' replied Rachel.

She had packed her best suitcase with carefully prepared clothes she thought she might need for her weekend with Adam.

Making sure she locked the door, Rachel stepped up to the beautiful car. The driver took her luggage and held the back door open, averting his gaze as she climbed into the car.

"Good evening Madam" he greeted politely.

"I'm sorry, I don't know your name" she said.

"It's Carmichael, Miss", adding with a chuckle "Yes, I know!"

"I don't stand on formalities", laughed Rachel. "What's your first name?"

"Michael, Miss". Honestly.

They both burst out laughing.

"Well Michael Carmichael", chuckled Rachel, "I'm delighted to meet you! And thank you for coming to collect me. Getting round the M25 at this time must have been a nightmare!"

"This one is really nice" thought Michael as they chatted easily on the journey. "Much nicer than some of the weird ones who visited Adam". But he kept his thoughts firmly to himself of course.

It was pretty much stop start all the way, but it was still only 8pm when they pulled into a long gated and gravelled drive.

'Wow!" exclaimed Rachel out loud when she saw the impressive grounds with a huge house at the far end.

"Nice isn't it?" said Michael. "Mr De Vere isn't, shall we say, short of a bob or two!".

The car crunched to a halt. The front door opened, and Adam stepped out to greet her. He threw his arms round her. He had really missed her. And she him.

"OK, Michael – thank you", he said. "As a reward, you can have most of the weekend off now. But we'll need you back here Sunday evening to take Rachel home. Is that OK?"

"Thank you, Sir. Will about 8pm be OK?"

Adam looked at Rachel who nodded. That would give her enough time to prepare for work on Monday.

"Yes, then" said Adam. "We'll call you if that changes. Have a good weekend!".

The Bentley drove off.

"Welcome to my humble abode" joked Adam. "Please come in"

"Thank you. But what if we need the car over the weekend? How will we manage?", Rachel asked innocently.

Adam laughed lightly. "We'll just have to use one of the others".

"The others?" said Rachel.

Cars were one of Adam's 'things'. He was pretty much a petrol head. "I'm going to have to show you what I mean" he said.

Dropping her case in the hall, he led her by the hand to the garage door at the back of the house. He threw it open.

The garage was almost as big as the house itself. And it was full of the most beautiful cars, old and new. There was an Aston Martin, a Ferrari, and a Lamborghini for starters. All immaculate. And all standing amidst other, precious cars.

Even Rachel, who knew nothing about cars, was hugely impressed.

Adam knew it was showing off a little, but he wanted Rachel to know everything about him. So that, soon it would all become normal to her.

He pulled her to him in the cool of the garage and kissed her long and hard. She welcomed the kiss

"And maybe that's not the only way I'm going to have to show you what I mean"

Rachel almost swooned. How had this man had such an effect on her?

"Let's take this back inside" she said unsteadily. They walked back into the entrance hall and kissed again. Wow.

"I think we'd best take your case up and I'll show you to your room so you can settle in". He disappeared off up the galleried stairway, carrying her case.

She followed, still a little unsteady.

"Will this one do?", said Adam as he threw open the door to a huge bedroom.

Rachel looked around. There was a huge bed, an en-suite with bath and shower, his and hers sinks. The bedroom was tastefully furnished but very modern. It was beautiful.

"That is fantastic – lovely" she replied.

But Rachel was rather hoping she wouldn't be using the gorgeous bedroom that night.

She wanted – no needed – him to fuck her. In any way he chose, she was game.

She'd work on that during the evening ahead.

Chapter Twenty

Alone at last

Back downstairs, Adam offered Rachel a glass of champagne. She noticed the chilling bottle of Cristal and gratefully accepted.

'This man is too perfect!', she thought to herself.

"I have ordered in a little dinner, is that OK?" Adam said.

"Lovely"

"I thought we could talk about how we can make this all work for both of us while we eat?"

"I'm so excited I'll get indigestion!" Rachel replied.

"Me too. Honestly. I haven't been this excited; felt like this since, well, forever!"

Dinner was being delivered at 21:30, so they had plenty of time to start their discussions early.

Rachel told Adam about her life. She didn't leave much out – boyfriends/relationships, work, money, travels. It poured out of her. She also told him she'd had a pretty conventional sex life, but since she had discovered his little kink, she had embraced it and was keen to try it out.

Adam's turn. He had been married twice, but neither marriage had worked out. Probably him being controlling he reasoned. He didn't know exactly how much money he had accrued. Although he knew it was well over £1 billion, some of it was tied up in assets. He owned places in New York, Madrid and had a pied a terre in central London. He had a beach house in Barbados too.

He owned all those lovely cars, but he also had a private jet, based not far down the road at Biggin Hill airfield.

He didn't have a yacht.

Adam's parents were both dead. They died in a tragic accident – a car crash – some years ago. He had no siblings and had inherited a large sum of cash from their will.

"So that's got all the flash bits out of the way!" he laughed.

"I also have a healthy interest in spanking young ladies. I expect you may have noticed?", he Joked.

"Noooo. You? A kink like spanking? I'd never have guessed. Good God! What is the world coming to?" teased Rachel with a huge smile on her face.

"Well should we save the rest for dinner, or should I tell you a bit more?"

"More please", said Rachel.

"OK, well I have to tell you this. I have had plenty of girlfriends and plenty of spanking relationships", he started.

"I need any relationships to be like this. I will be in control. I enjoy two types of spanking. First there is the erotic where I decide I'm going to spank you. If it's this mood I'm in you'll probably get a sound spanking and – I hope I'm not being presumptuous – I will then make love to you. Gently and slowly.

But then there is the angry. It doesn't happen too often but if I'm in this mood – and it doesn't have to be related to something you've said or done. It could just be I've had a terrible day at work, and you have only committed a minor infraction. Or it could be that you've behaved really badly in my eyes. If I'm in this mood I WILL blister your butt, make no mistake. Canes, crops, straps, restraints anything goes. And afterwards I will bend you over anything to hand and fuck you hard and fast, not bothering about your feelings and needs.

There, It's all out in the open now.

I hope I haven't put you off, but if I have it's best to find out now.

If you don't like anything I said I completely understand. You can have dinner and then go to your bedroom. We can have a vanilla weekend and then part ways.

I KNOW that what I'm asking is neither reasonable nor fair. I KNOW that others regard it as kinky.

But it is a huge part of me. One which I can't do without.

Maybe you'll have a think over the food?".

Rachel nodded. There was nothing Adam had said which was a surprise. The only minor issue was what if she wanted a spanking, but because of Adam's mood was given a thrashing? She wouldn't be able to earn just a spanking reliably. She would need to try and judge his mood.

The doorbell rang. It was the food.

Adam had ordered a Szechuan feast for four people! There was a mountain of food with all sorts of options: Duck, Chicken, veggie, and Vegan options. Lovely.

But, knowing what she was about to commit to over dinner, Rachel wasn't really hungry.

What she really wanted wasn't on any menu.

They put the food in dishes and ate with chopsticks. Rachel wasn't very good with them, so it was just as well she wasn't too hungry.

"OK, Adam", she suddenly said. "I listened carefully to what you have said. I have a couple of things to say myself."

"Go ahead, please", said Adam

"Well first please never embarrass me in front of others. If we are out, for example, and you are going to take me home for a spanking, then PLEASE don't tell the world. That would be between you and me and no-one else".

"OK, yes agreed. Absolutely" replied Adam.

"What's the second thing".

"Well, I have been naughty this week. Nothing too bad, but I have been swearing a bit recently. I think I could do with some correction to make me think about my language".

"I see. Well young lady. I think you'd better go up to your bedroom and wait for me. I don't like unnecessary bad language from ladies".

Rachel discarded her chopsticks and pushed her chair back. She pushed her chair back. She kissed Adam as she walked past him on her way to the bedroom. No going back now, not that she wanted to.

Rachel waited in the bedroom and stood when she heard Adam's footsteps coming up the stairs. She had those butterflies again.

Rachel was both a little relieved and a little disappointed at the same time. He had nothing in his hands.

He went straight to the comfortable armchair in the corner of the bedroom. He sat down.

"Come and sit on my lap please Rachel", he ordered. She obeyed.

Rachel was wearing tight, stonewashed jeans with hugged her bottom deliciously.

She sat on his lap.

He kissed her hard.

She could feel his erection though her jeans.

As she kissed him back, Rachel slid her hand up his thigh, first gently touching and then rubbing his rock-hard penis. Her hands moved towards his flies.

A firm grip clasped her hand.

"Not quite yet, young lady. There's the little matter of your swearing to deal with before we move on to THAT".

"Yes Sir", mumbled Rachel, almost bursting with excitement at the thought of exactly what was to come. She would be spanked for her bad behaviour. She deserved it. More than that, she wanted it.

Adam flipped her over his lap with one easy, no doubt well-practised movement.

"Are you ready to begin Rachel?" Adam asked formally.

"Am I ever Sir!" responded Rachel, smiling.

He started spanking her jean clad bottom. Ow! It was quite hard she thought.

That didn't last long.

"Stand up Rachel!"

She stood up.

"Now strip to your bra and pants. I can't get my message across with you getting protection from those jeans", he remarked. "So we'll have them off please"

Rachel complied immediately. Even though she had never been undressed in front of him before, she had imagined this moment so many times.

Adam thought she looked gorgeous, standing there in her white undies.

And then he bent her over and proceeded to give her a sound spanking, all over her bottom.

She kicked and squealed out loud before she felt her pants being slid down, slowly to the floor.

Adam continued. A little harder than before.

Rachel didn't understand why, but this was deeply sexual.

He slowed down the pace of the spanking. Rachel relaxed into it.

His hands wandered over her well spanked rear and gradually the smacks turned into rubbing. From bottom to rubbing her thighs. Gradually letting his fingers wander. She reached behind her and undid her bra.

"Stand up" he ordered.

"Yes Sir" she replied.

Adam turned the chair round, so it was facing the corner.

He bent Rachel over the back of it.

Again she reached behind her and stroked his penis. This time he didn't stop her as she undid his flies.

Rachel felt Adam move right behind her. He kicked his trousers and boxers from around his ankles. He moved forward and thrust himself right into Rachel, who immediately arched her back and closed her eyes.

The spanking had made her so wet, so excited, that what seemed like only seconds after he had entered her, Rachel felt herself coming. Screaming, kicking, clawing. This time there was no doubt about it.

This was simply the best orgasm she had ever had.

They pulled the covers back and slipped quietly into her bed. They fell asleep in each other's arms.

Rachel knew, instinctively, she was home.

Chapter Twenty-One

There was still the weekend

They awoke with gentle sunlight filtering through the window. Rachel looked at her lover while he slept.

He was handsome and clean shaven. A strong jaw, a six pack and muscular arms.

She knew already that she was deeply in love with this man.

She would do anything he asked.

Anything.

If Adam woke and wanted to spend the rest of the weekend in bed, she would happily do that. If he wanted to invent some infraction or other and whip her until she bled, that would be alright too.

She was, in a word, hooked. She wanted to please this man, no matter what he decided. Rachel adored him.

Adam woke and she planted a kiss on his forehead. He went for a shower. As the water rained down on his head, he thought back to the previous night.

Rachel had blown him away. She was gorgeous, funny, elegant. And she had been completely complaint when the time came. Too good to be true – I've hit the jackpot here.

And at the same time he, too, had realised that they were made for each other. This one was most certainly a keeper and he vowed to do his absolute best not to mess things up.

Usually he didn't care, but Rachel was different. He too was in love.

So after their showers, they sat in the kitchen and drank coffee from the Gaggia coffee machine. It was strong and lovely. But even Nescafe would have tasted lovely on that morning of mornings.

She found herself smiling happily.

'If being spanked felt that good, it was surely an incentive to repeat the bad behaviour!', she mused. But didn't say it out loud.

Adam suggested they might have lunch in the local pub in Godstone. There were a few to choose from and they decided on the Hare and Hounds – a traditional country pub. It boasted a full menu or bar snacks.

The pub was a 20-minute walk away. It was a nice day, so they decided there was no need for one of the cars.

The couple, for that is what they were fast becoming, chatted, and laughed happily as they walked along the lane into the village.

They pushed open the pub door and entered the traditional pub interior. The hum of conversation, the smell of good food and beer. It was a good choice.

They found a table and Adam went to the bar to order drinks. A gin and tonic and a lager. He took them back to the table, together with two menus.

They sipped as the studied the menu.

"Would you like a full lunch or just a snack?", Adam asked.

Rachel had seen a few things she really fancied and so answered "Oh a full lunch I think, if that's OK"

"Of course. Have what you want.", replied Adam.

"I've got my eye on the minted lamb cutlets" said Rachel. "Or maybe the Red Snapper. I can't decide."

After a minute or two she finally decided.

"No. Definitely the lamb please Adam".

"Good choice", he answered. "I think I'll have the mixed grill", he said.

"You never know, I may need my strength later!", he teased.

"Then have two!", she replied suggestively.

Again, Rachel was amazed by her forwardness. Adam twinkled at her. She looked at him in the shaft of light coming through the pub's olde worlde bullseye glass windows. He was very handsome. He was elegantly clad, even in dress-down clothes. Well-cut trousers. Cashmere jumper. Expensive deck shoes. He had a little stubble this morning. It suited him.

Rachel inadvertently dropped into the conversation that it was her birthday in a fortnight. Adam secretly vowed to do something very special for this wonderful lady.

"I know this wonderful French restaurant" he told her. "Do you like French food".

"Well, I can't afford to go to French restaurants very often", she laughed. "But yes, I adore French food. Probably my favourite".

The birthday would fall on the Saturday, as luck would have it.

"Well, maybe you'll permit me to book something?", he asked.

"You don't need to do that", Rachel protested. "I'd be very happy with an Indian or something… especially if I could go with you, Adam".

She looked at him and felt love.

Adam locked on her gaze. He got up and walked round the table to her. He bent down and whispered in here ear, careful for no-one else to hear.

"Please don't eat too much Rachel" he said quietly. "Because when we get home I'm going to take you to bed. And I'm going to take all your clothes off, bend you over the bed and fuck you hard and fast. Like you've never been fucked before."

And with that, he went back to his seat.

She blushed deeply.

There was nothing to be said.

Rachel's tummy was turning somersaults. She wouldn't be ordering too much then. She was longing to get back.

"Shame we've ordered already" Rachel said. "We could have gone back now!"

"It will be worth the wait, young lady" he teased.

How do you chat normally after something like that?

Both Rachel and Adam buried themselves in the days newspapers, offered by the pub, while their food was prepared.

But for Rachel, it was a way of avoiding potentially awkward conversations. She was not at all sure that any conversation wouldn't be complete gibberish at that moment.

Food was served. The lamb pink and succulent, served with buttered new potatoes. The mixed grill was huge, with steak, a chop, kidney, gammon. It was served with triple fried, crunchy chips, good old onion rings, mushrooms, and grilled tomato.

"God!" remarked Rachel. "I wouldn't be able to move after all that!".

"You won't have to", remarked Adam.

Rachel smiled a knowing smile.

They decided against desserts but took a brandy and a coffee each to finish their meal off.

For a pub, the food was remarkably good. Reasonably priced too.

Adam paid the bill, including a good tip. Building the anticipation. He spoke unsmilingly. "Right young lady. It's time to get you home. Let's go".

Rachel stood and followed the impatient Adam to the door.

The strolled back to the house in an awkward silence. Rachel was so excited, she didn't trust herself to talk unless she was answering a question.

Adam was planning.

He wouldn't spank Rachel – she had done nothing wrong. But he certainly was of a mind to act firmly. There would be no foreplay, just a proper, thorough seeing to. She'd never experienced this before, so it should be interesting!

The door swung open. Dam indicated for Rachel to go in first. He shut the door behind them.

"I'm not in a patient mood Rachel", please go up to my bedroom and wait for me there in your bra and pants. Off you go. I'll be up in five minutes"

"Yes Sir", said Rachel, wondering if she was due a thrashing.

Rachel hastened up the stairs. She was bursting with anxiety and excitement.

Adam couldn't wait the full five minutes. He entered his bedroom to find Rachel sitting on the bed, clad only in her beautiful black lingerie. She smiled nervously.

"Stand up", Adam ordered.

"Yes, Sir". She obeyed immediately.

He walked over, wrapped Rachel in his arms and kissed her. Angrily. Passionately. Longingly.

As he kissed her, he undid the clasp on her bra. His hands wandered hungrily over her soft breasts. Her nipples were hard with longing.

In one movement, he took her pants off and turned her round. He placed two pillows on the end of the bed and bent her over. She thought her heart might burst out of her chest, it was thumping that hard.

He stood behind her and stripped completely.

Without a word, he stood between her legs, kicking her ankles apart. His penis was rock hard. He was going to enjoy this.

So was Rachel.

'Right' he thought and without further ado he entered her. He stayed still for a moment and then began pumping in and out of her at a fast rate. He fucked her furiously – like he'd never fucked anyone before.

Rachel was in ecstasy. Tearing at the mattress with her fingernails. He neither stopped nor slowed down. She couldn't help herself. Very quickly she came, but he still didn't stop.

He pounded in and out of her regardless and as he did so she came again. And again.

Adam couldn't stop himself now and he came inside her after she orgasmed for the third time. They collapsed with him still inside her. It was a lovely warm feeling.

Rachel had never had it like that before. And it was sensational. It was in complete contrast to their first time, yesterday. It had always been warm, sensual even. But this was something altogether different. Animal lust.

Later, after showering, they sat and watched TV, wrapped in soft, fluffy robes. They ate a sandwich for supper. Just like a happily married couple.

They were both very, very happy.

Sunday evening came all too quickly. Adam kissed Rachel tenderly as she left with Michael in the Bentley. They would miss each other.

"I'll call you tomorrow", he promised.

"You better had!" replied Rachel.

"And can you come over next weekend? Please? I have a big surprise for you" he shouted as she wound down the car window.

"Yes please!" answered Rachel.

"Are you OK, Rachel?", asked the chauffeur gently. He had noticed a little tear in the corner of Rachel's eye as they pulled out of the drive and onto the Surrey lanes.

"Never been better Michael Carmichael….. never been better".

And she had never meant anything more.

Chapter Twenty-Two

Planning Rachel's Birthday

The next two weeks were going to be a bit hectic for both Adam and Rachel.

He had to plan for her birthday.

She had to catch up with Angela.

Adam was totally blown away by the way things were turning out with Rachel. The pretty, witty girl who a few months before he hadn't even known.

He had never been in love before but this sure as hell felt like love.

He wanted to spoil her. Money meant very little to the billionaire, but what could he buy her.

It came to him suddenly. He'd buy her a car! Nothing ostentatious. Maybe a Mini. Rachel had told him that she had passed her test some time ago but had sold her old banger because it was falling to bits and costing her a fortune.

So he made a few calls to BMW dealerships to check what they had in stock.

If it was to be a Mini, it needed to be the Cooper S – he knew that much. But as he spoke to dealers, they suggested the electric Mini. It was a quick as the Cooper S and had a range of about 125 miles. The local dealer didn't have any in stock, but eventually he found one at the Redhill showrooms – not very far away.

Michael drove him over to see it. It was gleaming white. Perfect. He asked if it could be delivered and how soon.

It could be delivered, subject to cleared funds, but it wouldn't be until the Monday.

"That's no good" Adam said. "It needs to be this week. I'm prepared to pay the full price today, no haggling. I'm only in Godstone. Can anything be done?".

"Let me check, Sir."

"OK, but I will walk away from the deal if you cannot deliver this week".

The salesman returned shortly, having consulted his manager. Sales were pretty slow at the moment. He smiled broadly.

"Sir, would tomorrow do? We need a little time to do the pre-sale checks, but we could deliver the car tomorrow afternoon?"

"Ideal" said Adam. I'll transfer the funds now. What are your bank details please?"

The salesman provided the bank details but wanted to check the price. The model they had in stock had been ordered for someone else, who had subsequently cancelled. It had every extra going and so the price needed checking carefully.

"May I suggest you give me an hour and I'll call you with the final invoice amount. You transfer the money, and we'll deliver tomorrow?"

"Yes, that will be great".

Adam gave the salesman his number and returned home.

Before the hour was up, his phone rang. It was the salesman.

"Sir, the overall price is a little over £45,000. Shall we call it £45,000 exactly?"

"Right. I'll transfer to money within the next five minutes. If you could confirm once it's received, please? A text would do fine."

"Certainly Sir".

Adam transferred the money.

The salesman texted to confirm receipt.

Adam was pleased with the service he had received and told the salesman so in a texted reply.

The next afternoon – the Tuesday – the Mini was delivered, fully charged and ready to go. It gleamed in the sunlight.

Adam completed the necessary paperwork and the flatbed delivery transporter duly left.

Adam and Michael took it for a spin, tried out all the controls and decided it would be a fabulous present. Even Adam, who could afford any car he wanted, was impressed with it.

They topped the charge back up and parked it round the back of the house.

Exciting.

Meanwhile, Rachel was back to work on the Monday morning.

One of her colleagues remarked, "Well someone looks like they had a good weekend! You're smiling from ear to ear!"

"It was nice thanks", Rachel replied. But didn't elaborate. If only they knew.

The housing market was still a little slow and so the days passed slowly. Time always passed more slowly when the market was down.

She phoned Ange and they arranged to go for an Indian meal on Wednesday. Rachel could bring her up to speed on how things were going. And Ange had a secret she had decided to share.

They were good friends. Rachel was a little sad as she realised she would have less time for Ange now she was in a relationship.

But what a relationship. She was absolutely certain it was love. Should she tell him so?

Probably not.

Ange and Rachel shared a lovely sit-in Indian meal. Actually it was Bangladeshi cuisine. The food was lovely, if a little too hot for Rachel, but delicious all the same.

Rachel told Ange all about her special weekend. She didn't leave too many details out, it's fair to say. How they'd agreed on some punishment details for the future, how they'd eaten, how they'd made love – once lovingly and once being well and truly screwed.

In truth Ange was a bit jealous. It could have been her with this too-good-to-be-true guy! But she was pleased for Rachel, and she said so.

Once Rachel had told her story, it was Ange's turn.

She admitted her thought process to Rachel. How punishing her had invoked strong feelings which she wanted to explore. How she had advertised and located a suitable responder. How they had had coffee and dinner. How she had given Jane a good hard spanking. And how they had agreed to do it each month for the foreseeable future.

In truth, Rachel was a bit jealous. Her best friend was reaching out and experimenting with someone else. Spending time with a new friend. But she was quietly pleased for Ange, and she told her so.

The rest of the week dragged until, at last, Michael was outside her flat on Friday evening.

"Evening Michael", said Rachel with a huge smile.

"Evening Rachel", he smiled back. "Have you had a good week?"

"A bit boring really", she replied.

"Well, I have a feeling that's all about to change", said Michael mysteriously.

"What do you mean, Michael?", asked Rachel, her curiosity piqued.

"Nope. I'm not saying a word. You'll have to wait and see for yourself", laughed the driver.

Rachel was excited now.

Not long to find out.

Chapter Twenty-Three

The gift

Rachel leaped out of the car, thanked Michael, and threw her arms around Adam, who had come out to meet her.

It seemed ages since she had last seen him, but in fact it was only five days.

They kissed, passionately.

"Hmmm. I think you had better come inside!" he teased.

"Yes" she enthused. "Where do you want me?".

Right at that moment she would have done ANYTHING for Adam's happiness.

"Whoa, whoa!", laughed Adam. "Slow down for a moment!."

He handed her a glass of 2007 Chateau Margaux, premiere cru. Adam had a refined taste in wine. It was from a bottle worth around £500. He knew Rachel preferred white wines, but he wanted her to try this special red.

And she loved it.

"Wow!" she exclaimed. "That's lovely! What is it?".

"It's very special, that's what it is."

"It's gorgeous".

"Rachel, I want you to come with me.", Adam said seriously.

Rachel thought she might be in for an immediate spanking. 'Ah well' she mused. 'He sounds very serious. I might be in for the painful one this evening. No point in worrying now'.

He took her firmly by the arm and led her through the kitchen to the back of the house. To her surprise, she found Michael there, carefully polishing a gleaming white Mini.

"I haven't seen that one before" she remarked. "It's a beauty".

"You think so?", asked Adam.

"Oh yes. When I had a car it was a Mini. I really like them. Is it yours?" she asked.

"No", came the reply.

"It's yours. Happy Birthday!"

"What? I don't understand.... What do you mean?"

"I bought it for you. It's electric. It will easily get you to Hillingdon and back and will be great for whizzing around London in".

Rachel was dumbstruck. She accepted the keys from Adam, not believing it was hers. She cried.

Adam was delighted with her response.

Michael too was pleased for her. She was a lovely girl, both in looks and in personality. If anyone deserved a present like this, it was Rachel.

"It's taxed and I have, for now, covered you on my insurance until we can get it all sorted. So go on – take it for a little drive."

"But it's not my birthday until next weekend" Rachel pointed out.

"No, but I have another surprise for next weekend. Go on darling. Have a little drive before dinner".

Darling! He had called her darling! Was it a slip of the tongue? She hoped not.

He pressed the keys into her hand and opened the car door for her.

Unbelieving, she climbed into her new car. It was fabulous. She adjusted the mirrors and the seat. She started the engine and tried all the gadgets. It had air-conditioning, a state-of-the-art sound system and lots, lots more. Almost every gadget she could think of.

Rachel shut the car door and gingerly drove down the drive. She was in a daze. It was so lovely. And it was HERS!

She didn't go very far. She was a little nervous and afraid of damaging it! Wait til Ange saw this!

Thoughts flashed through her head. What would she tell the girls at work? How could she possibly afford a brand-new car like this? They'd probably think she was embezzling!

The Mini soon became comfortable to drive, if very fast to accelerate. Before ten miles, she was totally at home with it.

Brilliant! She'd better head for home though. They would be worrying about her.

So Rachel stopped, reset the Satnav she wasn't exactly sure of where she was!) and returned back to Adam's house.

She went back inside, careful to lock her new pride and joy.

Once back inside, she found Adam and thanked him with a deluge of kisses.

"Thank you, thank you, thank you!", Rachel enthused. "It's absolutely perfect. Are you sure, Adam? It must have cost so much money."

"Don't be ridiculous" answered Adam. "You're worth every penny. I would have paid double just to see that reaction on your face."

"It is so lovely", said a genuinely excited Rachel. "I can't believe it".

They finished their wine from a little earlier.

Rachel snuggled up to Adam on the sofa.

Soon they were kissing, breathlessly.

"Well, if you're not wanting to spank me tonight, I guess it's time I showed you just how grateful I am".

"Who said I wasn't going to spank you?", he teased.

"Well, are you Sir", she asked. Whilst undoing his trouser belt.

"Not just at the moment", he replied.

So she continued undoing his trousers, rubbing his erect penis, and then sliding her hand inside his boxers.

As she gently masturbated him, she knelt down on the floor, between his feet. She tugged his clothes out of the way before starting to gently lick and nibble his penis and balls.

She suddenly took it in her mouth and began running her tongue up and down the shaft.

Adam sighed in ecstasy. And placed his hands on her bobbing head.

Rachel could feel him coming. She had given blowjobs many times before, but she had never allowed her partner to come in her mouth.

She decided she wanted to this time.

She upped the speed and sucked hard, flicking her tongue lightly as she did so.

She felt him tense as his grip tighten on the back of her head. A hot spurt hit the back of her throat. She sucked and licked until Adam was totally drained, milking his balls to ensure he had finished coming. It wasn't as unpleasant as she expected.

"Oh God Rachel. That was so fucking nice!. Thank you, darling!"

There it was again!

She was going to have to talk to him about this.

They ordered in Thai food and, after eating, they snuggled upon the sofa, just like any couple in love.

"Adam", started Rachel, "we can talk about anything can't we? I mean we get on so well?"

"Yes, sure" replied Adam. "What's on your mind?".

"Well, twice this evening you have called me darling. Was it just a slip of the tongue? "

"No. I called you darling because I feel very strongly about you. I know it probably sounds ridiculous after such a short time, but I have never had this sort of feeling before. Ever. Rachel I think – no I'm sure - I've fallen in love with you."

Rachel let herself breathe out. "Oh, I'm so glad you said that. I feel exactly the same way. It DOES sound ridiculous, but I love you too Adam".

They kissed.

They watched a bit of TV.

But they couldn't keep their hands off each other.

"Fancy an early night?" said Adam.

Rachel didn't need asking twice.

"Your room or mine?", she said as Adam chased her upstairs

Adam playfully slapped her bottom as he chased her. She grinned.

"Get to my room, now!", he ordered, playfully.

So she did, shedding clothes as she went.

The next day dawned and it was sunny. The leaves were beginning to turn brown now as Autumn loomed, but it was a beautiful morning.

Over coffee, Rachel asked Adam if they could go to the pub again for lunch. She had enjoyed that last week. Adam agreed, but suggested they try a different pub this week. Godstone had a number of lovely pubs.

Rachel wouldn't be able to drink alcohol this week, as she would be driving home in her wonderful new car, so she offered to drive them when the time came.

She parked the Mini at the front of the White Hart and they went inside to find a table. It was a little quieter than the pub they used the previous week. They ordered drinks and settled to look at the menus.

Rachel decided on the grilled fish. Adam the Ribeye steak.

"Getting your strength up for later?" she teased.

"I haven't decided that yet" came the unsmiling reply. "So don't be cheeky". He held her gaze. Best not poke a stick in THAT hornet's nest!", she mused.

As they waited for the food, the conversation turned to travel. Adam had travelled extensively. He had a beach house in Barbados whish he frequently travelled to, but he had been all over the Caribbean and the Indian Ocean. He had travelled to all the major cities. The Great Barrier Reef, Cape Town, Calcutta (he could never remember it's new name) – you name it, he'd been there.

Rachel, on the other hand hadn't travelled much. She had been to the usual European holiday haunts and on one trip to Egypt with Ange, but it didn't add up to much.

"OK" Adam ventured. "How about I take you up in my private jet next weekend, for your Actual birthday? We won't be able to land anywhere, but you'll love the experience I'm positive."

"Really?!" said Rachel, loving the idea. "Are you a pilot then?"

"Oh no" he laughed. "But I can wear the uniform if you like! I have a pilot on standby. What do you say?"

"Yes please!", said Rachel, feeling thoroughly spoiled.

"Will I need to bring my passport or anything?".

"Technically, the answer is no as we're not going to land anywhere", lied Adam. "But it will be easier if you do. It helps with the pre-flight paperwork and formalities" said Adam as if he had been asked this a hundred times before.

The couple chatted happily over their beautifully prepared lunch. Again they scanned the pub's Sunday papers. Again they contained mostly gossip.

Adam asked her if she had anything to tell him.

She looked at him, puzzled.

"I'm asking how you have been behaving since your last spanking", he said in a low voice.

"Oh!", said Rachel. She had been taken by surprise. Actually she had made a mental note of things which might be adjudged bad behaviour.

One little jokey swear which had popped out as she was chatting with colleagues; she wasn't sure if calling one a bastard in jest actually counted. One time late for work. Nothing much else. She recounted these to Adam.

"I see", he said weightily. "Not much better then. I think I will take you home to address those. Nothing TOO bad, but I think you need a little reminder, don't you?".

"Yes Sir", she replied. Inwardly delighting at the prospect.

"Right. You had better take us home now, I think".

"Yes Sir"

Rachel drove the short distance home, squirming. She plugged the car in before entering the house. She would have to get used to doing that.

Adam was already sitting on a dining chair, right in the middle of the living room.

Rachel was relieved it was only going to be a spanking.

She hung up her oat, put down her bag and instinctively walked to his right side.

"No Rachel. You will go upstairs to my bedroom. You will see a large cupboard behind the door. It's not locked. From inside the cupboard, you will see a small riding crop. Bring it to me".

"Yes Sir. Replied Rachel, obediently. 'Uh-oh!' she thought. 'It sounds like a whipping after all'. Ah well, it couldn't be helped.

She climbed the stairs and went into Adam's room. She opened the cupboard and gasped. Inside were a large selection of implements which she had no doubts that, in time, she would feel across her poor bottom. There were blindfolds, gags, and whips too. Oh my God. Would she be able to stand this?

Remembering the time, she located a small riding crop. As an afterthought, she also selected a silk blindfold and some handcuffs. She closed the cupboard and raced back down the stairs, her heart thumping.

She handed the riding crop to Adam.

"Sir, I thought you might like to use these on me?". She handed him the cuffs and the blindfold.

He took them but didn't say a word.

Adam stood up. He slowly walked around Rachel. He kissed her deeply. And then began undressing her. First, he gently pulled her jumper over her head. Then he fumbled with the metal button on her faded jeans. They were difficult to take off. Then her bra. She stood in front of him, nipples erect and ready.

He gently placed the folded silk over her eyes and tied it in place. He put her hands in front of her and handcuffed them together. She was now feeling very vulnerable. But bursting with excitement at what her punishment would be.

"Sir?" she said.

"What is it?"

"I want to say sorry for my repeated bad behaviour. I am ready to be punished as you see fit. As long and as hard as I deserve, Sir. Thank you Sir".

Adam was in two minds now. He had not intended to really punish Rachel hard, but here she was – asking him to do it.

He made a decision. Rachel would not dictate the terms of the punishment. That was for him to decide. He would carry on as he had originally planned.

Adam placed a cushion on his lap, so the handcuffs would not dig in. He then pulled Rachel towards him and kissed her again. And then pulled her over his lap.

He took his time before laying the crop on her bottom, teasing. She clenched her bottom as it lifted from her skin. But he was teasing again. A few moments later, he brought it down firmly on her ass. Not TOO firmly, but enough to make Rachel jump.

"I think I will give you three dozen like that" said Adam matter-of-factly.

"Does that count as one?", said Rachel cheekily.

THWACK!

"No, and neither does that!" said Adam, having whipped her bottom harder for her teasing.

"Are you ready, Rachel? This is for continuing to swear and being repeatedly late for work".

"I'm ready Sir" she replied, rather too eagerly.

"No you're not!", Adam replied, deftly removing her pants.

And so she was given 36 more strokes of the leather crop. Hard, but not viciously. It didn't break the skin but neither he nor she cared if it did.

Rachels bottom was very sore, and she ran her fingers over the welts and whip marks as she stood up.

The cuffs and the blindfold had somehow added an extra level of kinkiness to the proceedings. She couldn't anticipate when strokes were coming. She couldn't protect herself from the pain. The vulnerability somehow heightened the sensations.

But most importantly, she had pleased her partner. Removed any anger or annoyance he had with her. Pleased him.

Adam uncuffed her. She took the blindfold off.

He threw her down on the bed and knelt between her legs.

He licked and tongued her to an intense orgasm. Breathlessly she came. Again and again.

This man definitely knew how to push her buttons!

A quick nap followed, after which they made a sandwich and watched a little TV, arms around each other. She felt a little guilty about being pleasured with nothing in return, so Rachel reached out for his penis.

She freed it and started to give him the best hand-job he had ever had. Slow and sensuous. Adam exploded in her hand before very long.

She felt better now.

So did he.

Once they had cleaned up, it was time to leave.

Rachel slid into her posh new seat with more than a little care. Adam slammed the door.

She tried to open the driver's window, but only succeeded in turning the wipers on! Both burst into fits of giggles.

Adam agreed to call with plans for the weekend. Again Rachel wiped a small tear away.

This felt good.

This felt right.

Chapter Twenty-Four

Angela and Jane again

Jane rang Angela's doorbell, more than a little excited.

She had some serious things to confess this month and was nervous about the response she would get.

"Come on up Jane", came Angela's voice from the tinny intercom.

Jane was an attractive woman with a lovely figure and Ange had looked forward to this day since they last met.

Jane knocked at the apartment door and was duly let in.

Ange hugged her.

"Right, Miss", she said. "Red or White?"

"White please" Jane answered.

They sat on the sofa, chatting.

"What have you been up to since our last meeting then Jane? Has your behaviour improved a little? It needed to!", said Angela

"I'm afraid I've done something terrible" But may I please have another couple of glasses of wine before I admit it to you? I have a feeling I'm really in for it tonight, honestly."

Angela poured her another large glass of wine.

"What is it you have done which is so bad then" Ange asked.

"Well" said Jane "I have cheated on my boyfriend. Well not fully cheated. I didn't sleep with the guy. But I went out on a date."

"I see!" said Angela sternly. "And exactly what did happen then?"

"We kissed. I let him feel my boobs a little bit but that was it. When he went to put his hand down my pants, I stopped him".

"Jane, that is absolutely disgraceful behaviour. There is no excuse. What, exactly, do you want me to do about this?"

"Umm. I know it's disgraceful. I should be horse whipped. I'm so upset".

"I don't have a horse whip, but I do have a stout cane. For this, I am of the opinion you should be punished extremely hard. Do you agree?"

"Yes Miss" was all Jane could think of to say.

"I think a cold caning on the bare bottom. It always hurts more if you don't have a warm up spanking. I'm thinking 24 of the VERY best. By that I mean as hard as I possibly can.

Jane gulped.

"But I need to be sure that you don't think this is excessive. And you think it is truly deserved. Well?"

"Miss, I have never deserved anything more in my life. Please discipline me so I don't ever do it again" pleaded Jane.

"I intend to", responded Angela, coldly.

"Now, come here. I don't intend to waste any time in making you very sorry for your behaviour".

Jane went over to Angela. She had chosen fairly formal clothes for this evening. A black, well fitted trouser suit paired with a tight cotton blouse. The trousers were tight across her bottom. She had treated herself to some new lingerie for this occasion.

Angela took her jacket and hung it up.

She unbuttoned Jane's blouse and placed it over the back of a chair. Then she undid the smart trousers, looking at Jane all the time. Jane avoided her gaze. Slipping them off with Jane helping by stepping out of them, she hung these up too.

Stand there Angela said, pointing behind the sofa.

Angela had a few canes to choose from but had no hesitation in selecting the thick, senior one she had hung in her wardrobe.

She meant business this time.

And Jane was ready and willing to relieve herself of some guilt.

"Bend over the back of that sofa and prepare yourself for a real thrashing".

Jane was already in tears, before it even began.

"If you jump up, or even move, I will begin the punishment again" said Angela.

Jane quivered. She felt vulnerable dressed only in her bra and pants, but she knew that this was well deserved. And in not too long it would all be over.

She bent over, right on tiptoe, feet about eighteen inches apart. She grabbed onto the sofa cushion tightly, intent on taking her punishment without complaint.

Angela moved behind her. She slowly removed Jane's pants and Jane stepped out of them, kicking them to one side.

Angela had been cheated on by her last boyfriend. She knew just how hurtful this could be and she had finished the relationship. She was in no mood to go easy on Jane now.

She lined the cane up on the middle of Jane's bottom.

She took a step back.

She stepped forward and, without warning, cracked the cane very hard across the gorgeous, unblemished bottom.

Jane screamed.

Angela turned up the music.

A huge purple stripe had appeared.

Angela stepped back and repeated the dose, as hard as she could. The cane whipped into Jane's bottom. Again she screamed.

Angela was unmoved. She was allowing about 30 seconds between each stroke. Once 12 were administered, she allowed a couple of minutes respite.

"Halfway now. You're doing very well, but I will be finishing the punishment in full, Jane, make no mistake. Do you think I am getting through to you?"

"Oh yes, Miss. It's agony", replied Jane.

"Good!" replied Angela, taking up position again.

She stepped up and swooshed the cane across Jane's bottom for the start of the second twelve. Frankly, she was amazed how well Jane took it, but take it she did. Although she did scream quite a few times.

Eventually the caning was complete.

As Angela rubbed cream into the welts and cuts, Jane sobbed.

"May I stand up now Miss?"

"Yes, Jane"

Jane dressed and stood in front of Angela.

"Miss, I just wanted to say thank you for dealing with me like that. My bottom is a mess. I will be bruised for w a couple of weeks. But I really do love my boyfriend and am thankful to have you to stop me behaving like that again. I think it's safe to say that you have taught me a really thorough lesson today. I am very sorry that is has been necessary, but it was well and truly deserved".

"Actions, not words, Jane!".

"Now, you have been severely dealt with. "I will see you I one month. We'll see then if your deeds are matching your actions. Now, I have been intensely annoyed by your disloyal behaviour to your boyfriend.

I don't want to spend any more of this evening with someone who I'm annoyed with. So get out, go home and behave properly."

"Yes, Miss. Sorry Miss."

"Go!".

Chapter Twenty-Five

Surprise

Adam phoned Rachel on the Tuesday. He had forgotten he had a business meeting on Monday evening, and it had dragged on.

By the time it had finished it was too late to call Rachel, so he texted.

'Sorry, in an important meeting. As it's late, I'll call you tomorrow. Xx'

Rachel was still awake, so she replied.

'In bed. Wish you were. Love you very much darling. XX'

Adam glanced at his phone and smiled. Rachel wasn't a slushy sort of girl, so these words really meant something to him.

On his way home, Adam told Michael his plan for the weekend. She had said she loved French food. He said he would book a French restaurant he knew. They would go up, on the pretence of a short flight, but they would land in Paris. The French restaurant would be one of the finest in Paris! And he would take her shopping in the afternoon so she should be able to pick up suitable clothes and shoes for the classy restaurant.

If things went well, he was going to ask her to move in with him. The Surrey house was empty without Rachel in it.

He asked Michael what he thought of the plan. Michael heartily approved. Both the romantic gesture and the moving in. He was impressed by how down to earth she was. And how beautiful she was. He even gave Adam his true feelings about it.

"Adam, I have known and served you for many years now. I have seen numerous women come and go. Some nice and some not so nice if I may say so. But Rachel is different. Classy. Honest. Strangely innocent. Beautiful.

I cannot imagine a better fit for you. Congratulations!"

"Thank you, Michael. That is a lovely thing to say – I really appreciate it".

And so it was that Michael became involved in the planning. He rang Biggin Hill and ensured the aircraft paperwork was in order and up to date. He advised them that Mr De Vere plus one would be travelling to Paris on Saturday morning, returning Sunday afternoon. He phoned the pilot and agreed timings with him.

He arranged for the plane be provisioned with good champagnes and wines.

It was only a short flight, but attention to detail was important here.

Adam hadn't had to do anything – he was in awe of his driver's organisational skills. He had been thinking for some time that Michael was so much more than just a driver. He would speak to him later and award him a substantial pay rise. Michael was already well paid by driver's rates, but he was doing so much more than just drive. He didn't, perhaps, live in the real world where people had to worry about mortgages and such things. Money meant very little to him. He decided to give Michael a £10k p.a. pay rise.

Adam phoned Rachel early on Tuesday. They chatted for a long time. About the new car. Rachel was really delighted with it. Her flat, though on the first floor, had one of the garages with it. It was just as well because that way she could charge the car. There was just enough space on the short drive to plug it in overnight. It was so quiet she remarked.

About her birthday trip. It was only a half hour or so flight, but she thoughtfully asked if she should bring anything with her. Adam told her 'Come as you are'. He told her the flight was arranged for 9am on the Saturday – her birthday – and that they should allow an hour before that for the paperwork. And to be sure to bring her passport or they may be refused permission to fly. He told her he had booked a really special French restaurant he knew for the Saturday night and that, as a birthday present, she could shop for a dress and shoes on the day.

She was excited. She had never felt spoiled like this before. And she loved it.

They hung up the call after eight. It had lasted two hours!

The week had again dragged on at work, but she had packed her weekend things in a small case an put it in the boot of the Mini. She drove it to work on the Friday so she could get off to a flying start after work.

Her colleagues all went to the car park to look at it. She told them she had got an amazing deal through a friend in Surrey. Well, it was pretty much true! Everyone loved it. Some were jealous.

Rachel set off a little early, as her work for the day was done. She motored out to the M25 and entered the stop-start traffic of the Friday night rush hour. She had set the inbuilt Satnav in case she didn't remember the turning off the M25 and the way from the centre of Godstone. She needn't have worried.

The drive took quite a while due to the traffic, but soon enough she crunched down Adam's gravelled drive and into his arms.

He had made a cup of tea, which she gratefully accepted and flopped down after the week's work and then the drive.

"How did she go for you?" Adam asked.

"Adam! You bloody wanker!", she exclaimed laughing, immediately regretting it.

"People who call cars 'she' should be shot! IT went brilliantly, thank you"

Adam was not used to being corrected. Less still to being called a wanker.

"That, lady, has earned you a good hiding", he responded, stony faced. "I won't spoil your birthday by dealing with your straight away but believe me there will be strict consequences before you go home."

Rachel felt the butterflies in her tummy start to stir. In truth, she was desperate to take the worst he could give her. She'd know that that it couldn't get any worse. She was dreading the moment but was actually looking forward to being harshly dealt with by Adam for the very first time.

"Sorry" she said quietly.

"Sorry what?"

"Sorry Sir"

"Better. Now put it to the back of your mind until Sunday. It WILL happen, I can promise you. You will regret that. You won't sit down comfortably for a week.", he added matter of factly. "I will make damned sure of that."

He was so masculine, thought Rachel. And as far as she was concerned, she had made a serious mistake. He could deal with her as severely as he wished. It was fair, and she wanted to make him happy. She shivered, involuntarily at the thought of it – a frisson of excitement!

Adam put it firmly to the back of his mind and told Rachel to make sure she did the same.

Neither was particularly hungry and so they made do with a sandwich.

Adam made sure that Rachel had her passport with her and checked its expiry date. He himself already had a small bag packed and checked.

To save time in the morning, they asked Michael to pre-load them into the Bentley. Rachel only just remembered to take out the clothes she would be wearing on the flight.

After a little TV, they decided on an early night. The couple slept in Adam's bed, just cuddling until they fell asleep.

The alarm sounded at 7am. It seemed like they had only just gone to sleep.

Rachel tumbled out of bed and through the shower.

Adam chose a shower in the main bathroom and did likewise.

By 7:30 they were in the kitchen with Michael, drinking the coffee he had thoughtfully prepared.

They both wished Rachel a happy birthday and gave her cards.

Rachel was excited. She had never been in a private jet before and didn't know quite what to expect.

Biggin hill was a small airfield where Adam stored his aircraft. It was a little over 11 miles door-to-door.

As luck would have it the traffic was very light on this Saturday, and they made the journey in twenty-five minutes.

It was a lovely, clear day. Michael went through the well-practised routine where he met the pilot and they filed the paperwork, flight plan and passport check together. Everyone at the airport knew and liked Adam, so it was really something of a formality. He and Rachel just had to show their faces before they boarded the aircraft.

Michael bade them a good flight and lied "I'll be here waiting when you have done". In fact he had been given the rest of the day off and would be picking up the couple until the next day.

The jet rolled to a halt, ready for them to board. It was a Cessna Citation CJ4. Originally its cabin had seated 7, but Adam had had it re-configured to a 4-seater for more space. More luxury.

It was stunning, with cream leather seats, wi-fi, TV screens for films, a bathroom complete with shower and a galley for preparing light meals. Rachel was stunned. Particularly when Adam produced a chilled bottle of Kristal for the trip.

Once they had settled and donned their seat belts, the jet taxied onto the runway. They took off into the stiff breeze and soon the ground slipped away below them.

The views were fantastic. Looking back towards London and down on the green Kent countryside.

Sipping the cold champagne, Rachel was entranced. She was hugely impressed by the trouble Adam had gone to for her.

She felt mischievous.

"Adam", Rachel said, "If you wanted to get into my pants, you really didn't have to go to all this trouble!" she joked

He laughed. "They wouldn't fit me!".

Fairly soon they were out over blues of the English Channel. It was time to come clean, thought Adam.

"Rachel…" he started. "You know how I promised you one of my favourite French restaurants tonight?"

She looked at him, puzzled.

"Yes?"

"Well did I tell you it was in Paris?"

Rachel was speechless.

"What? Really? You're taking me to Paris??" she squealed with delight. She had always wanted to go there.

"Yes", he grinned widely. "I have booked us into the Four Seasons Hotel and reserved a table in Le Cinq for 8pm.

"But Adam. Thank you so much - that's truly lovely, but I really only have the jeans and sweatshirt I am wearing!"

"I have taken care of that", smiled Adam. "And that's why we are going shopping this afternoon. To the Champs-Elysees. To buy you a new dress, shoes and a bag."

"Oh Adam! You are wonderful. Thank you. I could never have dreamed of this.".

"Let me read you the write up on the restaurant" said Adam.

"A Paris destination in its own right, Le Cinq by Christian Le Squer is synonymous with the apex of French modern and elegant cuisine, paired with the rarest wines selected by award-wining head sommelier Eric Beaumard. Its three Michelin stars are a reflection of the gastronomic experience of a lifetime – in one of the city's most majestic dining rooms.", he read from his phone.

"Oh that sounds wonderful!", exclaimed Rachel excitedly. "I can't wait!".

They enjoyed the rest of the short flight, just about managing to finish off the champagne before they landed.

Michael had sorted out an executive car to take them from airport to hotel and a uniformed driver was waiting as soon as the pair cleared customs.

Soon the couple were speeding through the busy Parisienne streets to the hotel. Before they knew it they were checked into a beautiful suite. Everything about this hotel was pure class, from the way they were greeted, the architecture, the beautiful fresh flowers. Adam wanted this to be a no expense spared day for his lover. And she was overwhelmed.

The room was gorgeous and, when Rachel threw open the French doors, she was stunned with the view of 'La Tour Eiffel', so close she felt she could almost touch it.

Never, ever had anyone been made to feel so special.

She kissed him.

"Thank you so, so much" said Rachel lovingly. "You know you don't have to do all this, don't you?".

"I don't have to, no. But I want to. And I can. I love you, Rachel".

A few strains of music filtered through the air.

They danced, deeply in love.

They enjoyed a fabulous brunch together and then went out shopping. Just round the corner to the Champs-Elysees.

All the big-name fashion houses were there – Vuitton, Gaultier, Gucci, Cartier. You name it and it was there.

"Do you like any particular label?" asked Adam.

"I've never been able to afford these types of clothes" said Rachel humbly. I feel a bit intimidated."

"OK, so first you need a dress, yes?"

She nodded.

Adam strode into the Chanel store confidently. He was approached by an elegant member of staff.

"My friend would like an elegant cocktail style dress. Black. Can you please show her some?

"Of course Sir. Madam what size do you take normally?. please come and sit whilst I fetch you some of our nicer dresses. Would you like refreshments while you wait?".

"No thank you" replied Rachel, growing a little more confident. "And I'm either and 8 or a 10 in the UK".

In a few minutes, the assistant returned and showed her the dresses. Some she thought were pretty hideous – all bows and frills. Some were fairly plain. But two looked stunning.

She tried them both on. She couldn't decide. Both made her look even more stunning than ever. Rachel tried looking for the price tags. There weren't any

"OK, let's look at a matching bag and shoes please to help us decide.", said Adam, supportively.

A few minutes later and the assistant returned. She had 4 bags and 4 pairs of shoes with her.

Rachel loved one pair of shoes in particular. Highish heels. Shiny black leather. They were undoubtedly elegant. And there was a bag – a small clutch bag – which matched the shoes perfectly.

"Right, wrap them up please", said Adam, proffering his Platinum card.

"Which dress did you decide on, please?", asked the shop assistant.

"Both" replied Adam simply.

"Adam! No!"

He leant close to her. "Yes!" he insisted. "And if you aren't careful I'll add arguing to the list of offences to be dealt with!"

She blushed. And she shut up.

They walked back to the hotel, stopping in the Dior shop to buy perfume. She tried a few, but asked Adam if he like the one she did – J'adore. He loved it. And he bought it.

Finally they called in to the Alice Cadolle store in Place de la Concordes.

"Time for a little present for me!", he laughed as he walked her into the lingerie shop. White was his favourite colour.

He chose her a beautifully simple bra and pants set. Just a little lacy detail. Lovely.

Now they really did struggle with all the bags. They half stumbled into the foyer. A bellhop took hold of them.

"I'll have them brought up to your suite, Sir".

"Thank you so much", said Adam, tipping him generously.

The couple went to the elevator and returned to their suite. Their purchases soon followed.

Rachel spread them all out on the bed. They were beautiful. She had done nothing to deserve them. But what if he thought she was a gold digger?

She worried.

She needn't have.

"Adam, could you please come in here?"

Adam came in and saw the lovely clothes laid out on the bed.

She was carefully hanging them all up.

She turned to him and said, plainly "Could I have my thrashing now please Sir?"

"What's brought this on?", replied Adam

"Simply that I adore you and that I upset you when you have been so nice to me".

"Well, I'm afraid you will have to wait young lady. I have been thinking about this. For your punishment, I will be needing a cane and a riding whip. I have neither here with me. It will have to wait."

"But what you can do, is give me one of your fantastic blowjobs before dinner. And I will be giving you a good hard fucking after dinner. I know you like it like that".

Rachel didn't need any further encouragement. She pushed him backwards, catching him off balance. She deftly took off his leather belt, thinking, 'I'll bet he'll be using that on me sometime'. She unzipped him and took off his trousers. She gently bit his penis thought the boxers for a while before whipping them off.

She at first liked up and down the shaft, very slowly. She milked his balls gently as she did so. Slowly, ever so slowly, she started licking the tip of his penis, nibbling at the foreskin.

And then she suddenly took the whole penis in her mouth, slowly moving her head all the way up and all the way down the shaft.

Gradually increasing speed, she bobbed her head fast now. Deliberate movements. Until she felt his balls twitch – any moment now.

Rachel slowed down again, sucking hard at the same time.

With a shout of delight, he came spurting his hot load into her throat. She didn't stop, continuing for ten seconds or so after he had come. Getting the last bits of his orgasm complete.

His head was spinning. He needed a minute to stop feeling dizzy.

Finally, Rachel withdrew her mouth. It was only a small thing, but it was a way she could repay him. And a way which she had grown to thoroughly enjoy. Win-win.

They lay dozing peacefully until it was time to get ready for dinner.

Adam had brought a smart suit and tie. Rachel had her new clothes.

Again they both showered and dressed.

Adam looked masculine and confident in his suit.

Rachel had decided which dress she preferred and dressed herself carefully. She styled her hair a little and then applied make up. She slipped into her undies and dress. She put on her shoes and transferred a few items from her old handbag to her new one.

She looked in the mirror. No doubting it, she looked – and felt – fantastic. The best she had ever felt. She was feeling SO confident.

Adam was wowed as Rachel came back into the lounge area of the suite.

"Will I do?".

She knew she would.

Adam offered her his arm.

"Would the lovely lady care for cocktails before dinner?" he asked.

"She would", smiled Rachel as together they went to the elevator and descended to the cocktail bar.

Heads turned as the handsome couple walked in.

Chapter Twenty-Six

Dinner in Paris

Adam had told Rachel all about the 'City of Lights'. If she wanted, they could do some sightseeing tomorrow. Maybe the Louvre? The Eiffel Tower? Maybe a Bateau Mouche trip on the Seine? The left bank?. He had timed the fight to get back late afternoon, so there would be plenty of time. For both sightseeing and dealing with Rachel. It would be a good day.

Rachel liked the idea.

They sipped cocktails before dinner in the cocktail lounge. Rachel loved the decadent feel.

"You know you are going to punish me tomorrow" said Rachel, quietly. She was thinking about it a lot, excited. "How bad will it be?". She squirmed.

"Very. The worst you have had so far. I don't put up with language and behaviour like that." Said Adam. He leant closer. "I am going to whip your bottom severely. And I'm not going to stop until I am satisfied.", he went on.

He knew instinctively she was turned on by the thought of this. And besides that, she truly deserved a proper thrashing. And, loveable though she was, he intended to whip her very, very hard.

Those butterflies again. She felt like a naughty schoolgirl who was being summoned to the headmaster.

"If it's going to be that hard", she said breathlessly, "could you tie me up so I can't escape?".

"I fully intend to. No-one could be expected to stay still for what I intend to do to you.", said Adam menacingly.

Rachel was a bit too scared to ask anything else. She still couldn't quite believe that she was somehow looking forward to this. He was going to take the skin off her backside and here she was, agreeing to it. Excited.

They ordered more cocktails and changed the subject. The city began to light up. The Tower looked spectacular as they made their way to Le Cinq, just before eight.

Wow! What a setting. The room was elegant and well-spaced out. The furniture exquisite and the view unequalled. It was perfect.

They were shown to their table and presented with the menus.

Rachel spoke a little French, but not enough to translate the subtleties of the menu, so Adam helped her.

Eventually they decided on the Asparagus with truffles and the Langoustines to start. They followed up with 'Blue de Chasey lobster' for Rachel and Lightly smoked eels for Adam.

It was normal in France to take a cheese course before, not after, the desserts so they chose a plate of regional cheeses, although they would not order them or the desserts just yet. And it was going to be the 'Iced dark chocolate crust' for both of them when the time came.

Adam asked the Sommelier's advice on wine. Some were hugely expensive – they had one bottle dating back to 1792, but he doubted it was drinkable now. The Sommelier asked what they had chosen to eat and then recommended a medium priced white. Adam ordered the recommended bottle and asked if another might be put on ice.

Adam was unsure if the restaurant had two or three Michelin stars, but it was certainly amongst the best in the world. And one of his favourites. He hoped Rachel would love it too.

Their meals were delivered at a leisurely pace, with impeccable service. Perfectly cooked and exquisitely tasting. Every mouthful was an assault on the senses.

The second bottle of wine was brought to the table, and – what with the after-dinner cognacs – Rachel was happily merry as they drained their glasses.

Adam leaned in. "Now darling, time for bed. Get back up to that room. I'm going to give you one last birthday present!"

Rachel got to her feet a little unsteadily, now anxious to get back to the room. Adam left a big tip and followed her.

The lift doors parted, and they were back in their suite.

Adam virtually tore his clothes off.

Rachel, touchingly, hung her new dress up carefully. She had never had anything this nice before and she was damned well going to take good care of it.

She stripped right down to her new pants. She looked gorgeous.

"Where do you want me?" she offered.

"Right here" Adam said, patting the bed beside him.

Adam was impatient. He had had a lovely day and now he was going to have his way with her. "I told you, hard and fast tonight is how it will be."

Without further ado, he tugged her knickers down, dropped his trousers and set about delivering on his promise.

Rachel was already wet, and he just placed his penis in the right place and slammed into her. No niceties. She liked it a bit rough, he had gathered.

He just pounded her, as hard and as fast as he could. Her face contorted with pleasure. He held her firmly by the shoulders.

"And tomorrow" he said without missing a beat, "I am going to take you up the ass."

Rachel didn't care about anything at all at that moment. Adam could do exactly what he wanted, and it would be totally OK with her.

Remarkably, he lasted more than five minutes at that frantic pace before he felt himself coming. At the last moment, he whipped his penis out and spurted over her erect nipples.

She had come twice in those five minutes. She felt complete.

So did he.

After showering together, soaping each other's back with the hotel's expensive toiletries, they fell asleep in each other's arms.

What a day.

The best day ever, Rachel decided as she drifted off.

Chapter Twenty-Seven

Home to Face the Music

Rachel and Adam enjoyed a light breakfast, still a little full from the previous night's dinner. Rachel smiled as she remembered the evening.

She wanted to see a couple of sites before they left, so first they queued for the Eiffel Tower. They went to the highest point allowed – the 3rd platform – and took in the panoramic views of the city.

They stopped for a refreshing limon pressé at a café on one of the wide Boulevards.

They went on to the Louvre and saw beautiful works of art. She had always wanted to see the Mona Lisa and was transfixed by the quirky smile.

They did the Bateau Mouches trip and that pretty much took their remaining time up.

Adam called Michael and asked him to liaise with their pilot and they made their way back to their glorious hotel.

Adam asked for the concierge to call them an executive car to take them back to the airport and settled his bill.

Rachel was absolutely certain it would be astronomical.

She was right, but such things didn't worry the billionaire.

Adam had bought Rachel a travel bag for her new clothes. She packed them carefully.

And soon the driver arrived, and they glided out to the airport in comfort at not long after three o'clock.

Arriving at the airport, things were a little more formal than at Biggin Hill, but the pilot negotiated most of the formalities for them.

Soon the plane was taxi-ing into take off position on one of the smaller runways.

It was a lovely day for flying and they would see all the sights of both Paris and London clearly.

They sat opposite each other, fastened their seat belts and the plane quickly climbed to cruising altitude. They glimpsed the Eiffel Tower on their left and the browny-blue shimmer of the Seine below them.

Rachel sighed. It had been a lovely thing that Adam had done for her, but now it was time to go home. Time to face the music.

She wondered how it was going to be – would she faint? And she had never been – how did he phrase it? – taken up the ass before. She was nervous about that too. But she had no say in the matter. Dam was the boss, and if he wanted that, then she would have to obey.

Rachel was keen to get her punishment out of the way. Excited even. She ran through what she thought would be the events of the evening to come so there would be no surprises in her mind. She was going to be well thrashed and there was no escaping that.

And all too soon, the small aircraft came to a halt at the Kent airport. They alighted, briefly showed their passports to the officials, and went outside to meet Michael.

"Good trip?", he smiled.

Adam looked at Rachel's shining face.

"You wouldn't believe it Michael!", she enthused. "Everything was absolutely perfect thank you".

"Fantastic", said Michael as he opened the Bentley's doors for them. "Oh, I remembered to charge the Mini in case you were driving home tonight Rachel".

"Ah! Thanks so much. I'd forgotten that!", said Rachel gratefully.

And very soon they were back at the house in Surrey.

Adam gave Adam the rest of the night off but told him he wanted to talk to him the next day.

"Absolutely nothing to worry about", he re-assured Michael. "In fact it's good news for you. Shall we say around three?"

"Fine", said Michael.

And he drove off.

'This was it', thought Rachel. She was really for it. "Can we get this over with please, Sir?", she asked.

"Go and get a shower", ordered Adam. I will deal with you when I am ready. "Come back here in just your pants" he said.

It was a little after five and the sun was setting.

Adam decided to do a bit of preparation for Rachel's punishment, retrieving the implements he wanted to use from his cupboard. He also retrieved a gag, a blindfold, and a few lengths of rope. He felt sorry for what he was about to inflict on Rachel, but no one must be allowed to get away with speaking to him like that. He was resolute.

It was nearly six when Rachel re-entered the room. She wore just pants, as instructed.

"Now!" said Adam. "You have been extremely disrespectful to me, haven't you Rachel?"

She was silent, head bowed.

"Haven't you Rachel!" he repeated.

"Yes Sir. Sorry Sir" she whispered. But she knew it was far too late for apologies.

"So I have decided to punish you in a slightly unusual way", he went on.

"In a moment, I am going to take you to the bottom of the garden. I am going to take your pants off, tie you to the table down there and beat you severely. We shouldn't be overlooked, but frankly I don't care if we are. Come with me!".

She hesitated.

"COME WITH ME!", he ordered.

It was quite dark now as they stepped into the garden. Rachel was quite glad of that as it meant neighbours were less likely to see.

She felt extremely vulnerable as they walked in silence to the old summer house at the bottom of the garden.

She spotted rough wood of the pub-type table at the front of it. She wandered if that was where she would be punished. She was quite excited and yet full of dread as Adam ordered her to stand by the table and wait.

He went into the summer house and lit a lantern, which he brought back outside.

"I will first blindfold and gag you. Come here!" said Adam in a tone you didn't argue with.

She did as she was told. First he tied a silk scarf firmly over her eyes. Next he produced a rubber ball gag"

"Please Adam! No gags. I'll be quiet.".

But Adam insisted. "Open wide!" he ordered.

She did and he put the ball of the gag in her mouth, fastening the straps behind her head.

"Good. Now bend over the bench. I don't want to have to tell you twice. RIGHT over and give me your arms one at a time".

Rachel didn't dare to anything other than what she was told. She was full of mixed-up excitement and fear.

Adam took her arms, one at a time, and secured them to each side of the bench. The rough wood of the table chafed on her tummy and breasts. It made no difference to a determined Adam.

"Now the same with your legs, one at a time".

Each leg was firmly secured to a table leg.

Finally, for good measure and to ensure Rachel could not move an inch, he tied one long length of rope across the small of her back.

He stepped back and was satisfied with his handiwork.

"Right. I know you have already been introduced to the cane before, Rachel. I intend to give you six of the hardest strokes for your insolence.

I don't think you have received the dressage whip before. It is about four feet long and is very thin. It has a metal core and a thin leather tip. Listen…"

Adam practised a stroke in the air. Rachel tensed as she heard the high-pitched whistle.

"After each cane stroke I intend to administer the whip. And lane it exactly on top of the cane stroke for maximum effect.

It is inevitable that it will cut your bottom in places, but that is properly deserved."

He reached down and slid her pants down as far as they would go.

Rachel was scared.

"Are you ready to be corrected?" said Adam

Rachel couldn't speak but nodded her head obediently.

Adam picked up the cane. He swooshed a couple of practice stroked in the air before taking up position. Accuracy was the key to making this the painful experience he intended.

He lifted the cane far above shoulder height and then brought it down with all his might. Rachel tried to scream but couldn't. He swapped the cane for the dressage whip, again lifting it above his shoulder. After a second, he cracked it across her bottom with a whistle and a crack. The whip stroke landed right on top of the cane stroke. Rachel had never felt pain like it. Adam looked on with satisfaction as he noticed the glistening around the cane mark on Rachel's poor bottom in the light of the hurricane lamp.

He proceeded to administer a real thrashing, covering her whole bottom with parallel lines, each with a glistening cut at the edge.

Rachel was distraught at first. She had never imagined such a beating and it was bloody agony. It was probably a good job that the gag had remained in place to stop her speaking to Adam whilst she was angry.

Slowly, he untied her ankles. He rubbed a little antiseptic cream into her bum. It didn't help much, if at all.

Next he removed her pants completely.

He took the blindfold and the gag off and then rubbed lubricant around her ass, inserting a finger to ensure she was properly lubed before dropping his trousers and closing up behind her.

"But Adam", said Rachel, between sobs.

"Be quiet Rachel. The worst is over".

And he pushed his penis right into her ass. She gasped.

He carried on. Another of those fast and furious fucks they both seemed to enjoy.

It was a new experience for Rachel, but one she found she didn't mind. Except for the hips slapping brutally on her thrashed backside.

Adam came very quickly. Rachel didn't make it. She wasn't used to the sensation. But it wasn't unpleasant. And Adam was being satisfied.

It was over.

Rachel didn't put any clothes on for the walk back to the house. She would need to address the wounds on her bottom before she could do anything. And she found she didn't give a fuck if they DID see her.

So what?

She went into the house and straight to the family bathroom.

She looked in the mirror at her thoroughly beaten bottom. He said he would do it and my God he did! Something deep inside her stirred.

She didn't know why, but she masturbated there and then, reaching a delicious climax very quickly.

She went back downstairs when she had showered. She took a towel to sit on.

"You OK" asked Adam?

"Just about" came the sullen reply.

Had decided now was not the best time to ask Rachel to move in, so he told her his other news, thinking it might cheer her up.

"Rach, I have news. I'm going over to my beach house in Barbados in three weeks' time. I thought I'd make it a holiday for a couple of weeks. Can you get the time off?".

Rachel was due some leave. They had to take it before January of else they would lose it.

She very soon brightened. "I'll ask tomorrow. Do you have exact dates", she asked?.

"Yes, I'll dig them out and text you them while you drive home", he said.

"It's Saturday to Saturday so it's whole weeks off work", he added.

It would have been impossible for Rachel to forget what a thrashing he had given her – it hurt way too much. But she was delighted with the prospect of a luxury Caribbean trip.

"Have you got any photos of your place over there?", asked Rachel.

"Sure, I'll send a few over with the dates, OK?"

Adam walked over to Rachel and wrapped his arms around her. "I really do love you, you know.", he said. "Despite how you need punishing sometimes".

She nestled into his shoulder. "I won't be doing that again, I can assure you!" she muttered, adding, "At least not for a while, anyhow!".

Adam applied more cream to her bum and provided her with a couple of clean towels to sit on.

Rachel stowed all her new clothes in her car and set off for home.

She hoped she didn't get stopped.

She was driving in her knickers.

Chapter Twenty-Eight

Discomfort

During the journey home, her phone pinged to notify her of a message from Adam, but she would have to wait until she got home to read it properly.

The drive home had been distinctly uncomfortable, but by the time she arrived she figured she deserved it. Fancy calling Adam wanker! She almost laughed.

Almost.

But her oh-so-painful bottom reminded her.

She pulled up on her own drive and plugged the Mini in to charge.

In the dark of the garage, she pulled her tight jeans on. It was agony. It took her an age to put them on.

She hobbled upstairs with her travel bags and went into the flat. As soon as she had done this, she took the jeans off and started running a bath for herself.

She threw the towels she had been sitting on in the washing machine and added some Vanish to the wash, which she started on a hot cycle.

The bath was only luke-warm. She added a little Dettol to the water and lowered herself into the water very gingerly. Oh how it stung! Her plan was to bring out the bruising quickly.

In the bath she looked at the text Adam had sent, as promised. He told here the flight dates – they were British Airways flights, two weeks on the following Saturday. That should be fine.

Then she turned her attention to the attached clutch of photos. His house looked great. She couldn't tell how big it was, but it certainly looked huge. Apparently it was right on the beach, just on the edge of Mullins Bay on the West Coast. The beach looked fabulous. The house appeared modern and comfortable. The huge private swimming pool looked inviting. And there was an outdoor kitchen, complete with BBQ. Rachel was already imagining diving into the pool and emerging to lovely smoky cooked food. It should be an idyllic holiday for them.

And she hoped her bruises would disappear by then.

She shopped for a couple of cheap sarongs, just in case. And two new bikinis. She had plenty of nice tops, shorts, and T-shirts. And now a couple of exquisite little black dresses for more formal evenings.

Rachel towelled herself and began to feel a little mor comfortable. She thought about her trip to the bottom of Adam's big garden. About how he was strong and gave her exactly what he had promised to do for her little outburst. And before she left the steamy bathroom, she found her hand moving towards her crutch. She couldn't explain it. She was still very aware of the thrashing she had received. But she still found it very sexy, even though this session had been severe.

Satisfied, she put a towel in the bed and laid down to sleep. But it hurt too much to lie on her back. She had to sleep on her front – a situation which would last for quite a few days yet.

She was tired after her French adventure.

Rachel soon fell fast asleep, dreaming of Barbados, pristine white beaches, brilliant blue seas.

The next morning she walked to work. She suffered with the stiffness in her bottom. She limped a little, but she managed.

She filled in a holiday request form at work which was duly approved and signed by her boss. She texted Adam the good news.

Adam texted back. He was delighted. His business was only for an updated residence permit, so they should have a nearly uninterrupted fortnight. There were things in Barbados which he really wanted to show her. Now he could.

Later that day he texted again. He had had a chat with Michael and given him a £10k pay rise, as he planned. Apparently, Michael was over the moon.

He was worth every penny of it and more, Rachel thought.

Adam was busy for the following weekend, so Rachel was able to arrange to spend a bit of time with Angela. She felt she had been neglecting her a bit. Besides, she had a lot of things to catch up with.

They arranged a night out on Friday and a pub lunch on Sunday. It would be great to catch up.

Adam was going to be busy for the next two weeks, so they arranged for Rachel to go over to Surrey to sort out holiday arrangements the week before departure.

Rachel did some holiday shopping locally – flip flops, toiletries, new wash bag and those sorts of things. She bought a new suitcase too. Nothing expensive, but her old one was falling apart and had to be held together by a luggage strap.

Pleased with her purchases, Rachel stayed in until the Friday on which she was meeting Ange. It was only a pizza and visiting a few local pubs, but Rachel was really looking forward to seeing her friend.

Ange turned up at Rachels at about seven. Rachel showed her the new car. Ange thought it was fabulous! "I'm not a bit jealous!", she said.

Rachel just grinned.

The friends walked to the local pub to start. They settled in the lounge with a couple of glasses of white wine and began chatting.

Ange told her about her blossoming relationship with Jane. Rachel asked her if it was more than just a spanking relationship they had, but Ange strongly denied there was anything more going on.

Rachel talked at length about their Paris trip for her Birthday the weekend before. It was hard not to sound like she was showing off to her friend, but she managed to maintain her air of down-to-earthness as she recounted the flight, the hotel, the shopping, and the dinner. She told Ange she could not believe how generous Adam was.

"He must be getting SOMETHING he enjoys!", giggled Ange.

"Well yes, but that works two ways!", said Rachel. "The sex is sensational!".

Rachel mentioned the upcoming trip to Barbados too. When she said it out loud, it all seemed to perfect to be true.

Ange was delighted for her, as any true friend would be. "Could've been me, that!", she joked.

"I can't believe how all this has grown", Rachel remarked. "I even enjoy the spankings! I honestly believe we're in love".

They drained their wines and moved on to the next pub, maybe a hundred or so yards further down the road.

They went through the same routine – more wine, more chatter.

Time moved on and they decided it was Pizza time!

There was an Italian place that did authentic wood-fired Pizza not far away.

The girls strolled there and asked for a table. They both ordered garlic mushrooms – well, Rachel wouldn't be seeing Adam and Ange wouldn't be seeing Jane before the effects on their breath had worn off. Sod it.

The followed up with one deep pan and one Calzone. One with Chilli oil; one without. They washed it down with cold Morettis.

And it wouldn't be a girls night out if they didn't have a dessert, so they ordered a sticky toffee pudding and a Tiramasu to complete the meal.

"Naughty but Nice! Just like you Rachel!" Ange remarked.

They laughed.

Rachel and Ange decided they would go back via the same route, stopping at the same two pubs to round the evening off.

By the time they reached Rachel's flat, they were a little worse for wear, so they said goodnight. They hadn't been out, out but they had certainly been out.

"Bring me back a stick of rock from Barbados", joked Ange.

Chapter Twenty-Nine

Planning the holiday

The days until she saw Adam again seemed to drag. Rachel loved his company, and she hadn't seen him for nearly two whole weeks now.

He had phoned her, of course. Nearly every day in fact. Sometimes it was just a quick call between business commitments. Others, it was a long, sometimes sexy conversation.

He had asked how her bottom was. It was healed now, but the marks and deep purple and yellow bruises were faded but still there after a fortnight. Rachel hoped they'd disappear in time for their trip. He said that Arnica cream should do the trick. He even offered to rub it in for her.

The weekend arrived. Rachel popped her iPad into the Mini, threw a few clothes together and set off into the traffic. She was going to be careful not to call Adam any names this week, that much was for sure!

Rachel arrived at Adam's place about 7:30, as usual. There were no big motorway hold ups.

They planned to make a list of things she would need for the holiday so she could shop for anything she didn't already have during the week.

Adam needed to nip out, briefly and asked Rachel if she'd be OK.

She assured him she would.

As he drove off, her thoughts wondered back to two Sundays ago.

She found herself walking in the garden, down to the summer house. She found it without too much difficulty. And there was the bench, over which she had so painfully been taken to task.

Rachel looked around, unnecessarily guilty. No one could see her. She took in the scene, remembering. Slowly undoing her tight jeans. She slipped her hand inside her pants and bent over the table. She took her top off so she could again feel the rough wood against her tummy. She closed her eyes, recalling all the sensations. Faster and faster she went, until she was bursting with lust. She didn't stop and enjoyed a blissfully long orgasm. She panted and she lay there, waiting for normality to return.

Slowly, Rachel got to her feet and adjusted her clothes.

'What a nice feeling', she thought. She found herself smiling as she went back into the house.

Just in time! She entered via the backdoor as Adam came in at the front. She was a little flushed.

Neither were particularly hungry, so Rachel prepared a favourite snack – cheese on toast. A good strong Coastal Cheddar on wholemeal toast. Lovely, they agreed.

Couple settled into a question-and-answer session as they ate.

"Will I need anything formal for the evening?", she began.

"Nope. One or two smart casual things in case we go somewhere posh", he answered. "But smart casual is plenty good enough for most places on the island".

"How about shoes?"

"Flip flops mostly. One smart pair of shoes. No high heels though. Maybe a pair of trainers if you have them? For walks and things", he explained.

"Great. I'm intending to take 14 T shirts, one for each day, and 3 or 4 pairs of shorts. Will that be enough?"

"Plenty!", he laughed.

"And bikinis. I think that's it then".

"I think you have forgotten something", Adam said. "What about underwear".

"Oh. Will I be needing any?" asked Rachel in mock innocence.

"On second thoughts, you're right!", said Adam.

They laughed.

She added underwear to her list.

Apart from the moments after she had been severely punished, Rachel and Adam were getting on famously. They were easy in each other's company. They were happy to be together without talking – reading a book; watching TV – it really didn't matter.

But tonight Adam had dug out more photos to show Rachel where she would be next week. Not photos of the house, so much. More photos of the island.

A steel pan band playing on the forecourt of a petrol station. The bustle of Bridgetown. Caribbean foods. Photos from the East of the island where tourists rarely venture – Bottom Bay, The Animal flower cave, Bathsheba, Crane Bay. Welchman's hall gully. Harrison's cave.

And then from the Friday night Fish Fry where locals and tourists mixed happily to the sound of reggae booming from the speakers.

Green monkeys living in the wild. He had so many of them.

Rachel was captivated. She had never seen such beautiful, empty beaches. Never known a place where you could pick up nutmeg and mace from the floor.

She had read that it was the most English of the Caribbean islands, but it all seemed a world away from Hillingdon!

It was nearly bedtime.

"Go on up please Rachel. Strip to your pants please", he said suddenly.

"But why? I haven't done anything wrong have I?"

"Don't question me please. Just go."

Rachel knew that her bottom was not ready for another thrashing, but she did as she was told.

She went to the bedroom and took off her pants.

Adam came up. "Bend over the end of the bed please."

"But Adam" she protested.

"It's OK, I only want to inspect that beautiful bottom for the damage I caused two weeks ago.", he smiled. "And I have bought you Arnica cream to finally bring out all the bruising."

She sighed with relief, bent over the bed, and slid her knickers down from her bum. "In that case, feel free".

The cane / whip marks were still visible, but they were fading from their worst. The cuts had healed and only a few small scabs were left.

The bruises were still prominent, but by no means as visible as a couple of days after the thrashing. They were all shades of blue, yellow, orange, and purple. She hoped the Arnica cream was good stuff.

Adam looked carefully. "Hmm. I think you may have learned a lesson there" he said quietly.

She had.

He tenderly patted and rubbed her bottom, ensuring every area was covered with the cream.

He gently took her pants off and turned her over to face him.

"How do you want it tonight? Fast and furious or slow and sensitive?".

"How about both? Slow and sensitive to start. And fuck me hard to finish", she said, with her eyes tight shut. "VERY hard".

Adam didn't need telling twice. He rolled on top of her and kissed her slowly. He gently cupped her chin in his hands. Then he ran his hands slowly over her entire body. He began kissing her all over, stopping here and there to allow more attention. He nibbled, gently bit, and grazed her gorgeous body. He licked and kissed her erect nipples. He flicked her clitoris with his tongue. She loved it and lay back enjoying the sensations.

Suddenly, after maybe fifteen minutes, he jumped up suddenly. He stripped in a second and immediately mounted her. She knew exactly what was coming as he at first lay still on top of her. Slowly, very slowly, Adam moved backwards and forwards. He gently slid his penis in and out.

Then he burst into life. He changed from sensual lover to animal, and he fucked her as hard as he was able. Plunging his penis right into Rachel before withdrawing it and doing it again.

Rachel found it remarkable that he could last five minutes of doing this without coming, but by the time he did, she had orgasmed three times. It was remarkable. Before Adam, she had barely had an orgasm and had felt forced to fake it on many occasions to make her partner feel good.

Not with this man! He was a stud. Rachel was totally drained. She fell asleep for a while, trying to decide if she liked the slow and sensuous as much as the fast and furious.

She had decided that, provided she was in the right mood, the hard and fast was better.

But it was close.

They did a bit of shopping on Saturday and managed to collect all the items on Rachel's list.

Adam had business related things to do on Sunday at around tea-time, so the couple decided to forego their 'usual' pub lunch and Rachel would leave early afternoon.

They arranged for her to return next Friday night with her cases. The flight was at 1:40pm on the Saturday, so they could start the holiday in a leisurely way.

They kissed and parted for the last time before their holiday.

Rachel was bursting with love and excitement.

She drove home, parked her lovely car, and began packing straight away. Some of the things she needed didn't need ironing, so they were packed carefully.

Others – toiletries – were wrapped in cling film, in case of leaks and placed in the case.

Her new bikinis, sarongs and one of the smart dresses could go in too.

Rachel went to bed that night with almost all her packing complete. Just a few more things to go through the wash.

And she packed her underwear.

Chapter Thirty

Arriving

Michael drove them to the British Airways check-in in at London Gatwick in good time for their flight.

Rachel shouldn't have been surprised by the fact that their tickets were First Class. She had never flown anything other than Economy class. This alone was exciting.

Their luggage was immediately checked in. They could have had much more, but only needed one case each. As First-Class passengers, they were taken via the hospitality lounge, where they passed the security checks and gratefully accepted the free glass of Champagne.

There were meals and snacks available. They both selected plates of canapes and happily settled into the plush lounge seats to await calling forward for boarding. Apparently, the aircraft would be leaving on-time. Great news as it meant, with a five-hour time difference and a nine-hour flight, they would be landing in daylight. And Rachel would be able to see the island for the first time from their carefully chosen seats on the left of the cabin. The prevailing winds meant that almost always the aircraft approach along the north coast, swinging left down the west coast to the airport. The views were fantastic.

First class long haul flights on BA came with seats which turn into a flat bed, but Rachel didn't want to miss a thing, right from the pre-take off Champagne through the in-flight entertainment, the meals, the wi-fi. Everything.

Adam, more used to travelling in luxury, would probably doze off after the meal.

They boarded at the front of the aircraft and turned left. She had always wanted to do that. The couple were shown to their seats and offered their champagne. It was ice cold and lovely.

Rachel read the menus for later. She loved her food and was pleased with the choices on offer.

She browsed through the 30 or 40 latest releases on offer and saw a few things she had wanted to watch but hadn't got round to.

She connected to the in-flight wi-fi. She would be able to collect emails and even maybe send one to Ange.

The seats themselves were wider and had more legroom than anything she had sat in before on an aircraft. And the flat bed would be useful on the way home when Adam had booked the overnight flight. They were very comfortable for aircraft seats.

This was fantastic.

Their flight took off bang on time and quickly climbed to cruising altitude. Rachel could soon see the little white puffs of cloud below them. It was a clear autumn day. The first-class seat configuration made it a little awkward when you were travelling with a companion. To give people some privacy, the seats were laid out to be private – to allow some sleep. It wasn't ideal when she wanted to point out every exciting feature she spotted to her partner. She managed though.

They ordered more Champagne and chinked glasses. "Happy holidays!", said Adam.

Both Rachel and Adam then sorted through the films.

Adam chose an all-action thriller.

Rachel chose a Rom-Com.

They settled down to watch their respective films.

Rachel found hers a bit frothy.

Adam's was all action without much plot.

They were glad they hadn't paid to watch them!

The Cabin crew kept them well stocked with drinks and came round for their meal choices.

Adam went for the Slow cooked British beef cheeks with Jalapeno potato gratin.

Rachel the duck in a wild cherry sauce with Parmentier potatoes and green beans.

All the choices sounded lovely.

Were no worries about drinking as Michael had arranged for them to be met once they arrived in Barbados. Adam kept a car there – a Range Rover, complete with removeable panoramic roof. He also paid a retainer to a property management company, who could supply drivers, cleaners, and chefs at short notice.

The meal was very acceptable. Not top notch but very tasty.

They chose another film, and the second choice was better in both cases.

They watched the flight's progress on the TV screen.

The made good progress and at long last the island of Barbados appeared on screen.

The captain illuminated the 'fasten seat belt' sign and began his descent. As Adam had anticipated, he flew along the island's north coast and then swept left down the beautiful west coast.

Rachel was stunned by the view she was afforded. The ocean was every shade of blue, the colours lightening as the water shallowed towards the beaches. She had never seen sea like this before. It was gorgeous.

The pilot announced that the local time in Barbados was just after 4:30 and the air temperature on the ground was still a lovely 29c. He told the passengers that he expected to be on stand ahead of schedule and he hoped we had had a pleasant flight.

First Class luggage appeared first on the luggage carousel, and the couple were soon clear of immigration and customs.

There, with a plaque held high, was their driver. The name "Mr A De Vere" on his board to confirm it.

They walked up to him and introduced themselves. The driver loaded their cases onto a luggage trolley and took the pair to the waiting Range Rover.

It had been a hot day and the heat when they walked out of the air-conditioning of Grantley Adams airport felt like a furnace blast when compared to the cabin and the airport. They fanned themselves as they walked to the car. The driver opened the door and started the engine so the aircon was working. They got in and the car began to cool down. The driver loaded the luggage into the boot and took the luggage trolley back before taking his seat.

He took the back road from the airport. First through fields of sugar cane before joining the Spring Hill highway up past the outskirts of Bridgetown. After a few miles, he dived down to the coast road and turned right towards Mullins.

Adam had seen the driver before, but he didn't remember his name. They soon re-acquainted.

And within 50 minutes of the landing, the security gates of a large house swung open for them.

Rachel thought how the photos Adam had shown her didn't do the house justice. It was set in tropical grounds with well-trimmed lawns. The building itself was of soft pink coral stone.

The pool seemed massive and had a lovely terrace surrounding it, complete with sun loungers, a table, and chairs. And the outdoor kitchen was huge! It boasted a sink for food preparation and a full-sized fridge.

As the gates closed behind them, a cheerful local lady greeted them warmly.

"Hello again, Mr Adam.", she said. "Hello and Welcome Miss....". And then she realised she didn't know Rachel's name.

"It's Rachel", she said helpfully.

"Welcome Rachel. I have made up the rooms as asked for by Mr Michael", she went on.

Rachel wondered if Michael had arranged for them to sleep in one room or two.

Turned out it was, as she hoped, one. The master bedroom at the front of the house. The one looking out over the pristine white sand to the aquamarine sea.

"I thought you would be tired after your long journey, so I have made pepper pot stew for you both. I hope that's OK. I have done a small shop and put breakfast things in the cupboard and fridge. And there's a couple of bottles of wine there too."

"Thank you so much Winnie!" said Adam. He generously produced a $50 US tip for each of them. The driver had a lift home from Winnie.

"If I could call you when I need you, that would be great. Well mostly be eating out, but I'm sure there will be plenty of times we need you" said Adam.

The couple slumped into the sumptuous sofa. Rachel was smiling.

"What a lovely place", she said. She was hugely impressed.

They unpacked their cases and hung-up clothes which they did not want to crease too badly. Rachels special cocktail dress. Adam's business shirt, suit, and tie.

Rachel flicked through the TV channels and found that it had all the English satellite channels.

Fuelled by Champagne, the rigours of the days travel soon caught up with them and they nodded off to sleep.

By the time they woke up, they tried a little of the pepper pot stew, opened – but didn't drink – one of the bottles of wine and then went to bed.. It was five hours later in their heads, and they wanted to be ready for a big day tomorrow.

"Adam?" said Rachel as they started to fall asleep.

"Yes?".

"It's nothing to do with what you buy me, or how rich you are. I honestly love you very, very much".

"That's how I feel too", he said honestly.

"I have an idea which I'll share with you during this holiday. Let's see what you think, eh?"

"OK. Night darling",

Chapter Thirty-One

Surf and Steel Drums

The next day was Sunday. The Jordan's supermarket was open in the morning, so after a coffee, they drove up the coast to Speightstown.

Rachel was surprised that they drove on the left and steering wheels were on the right, just like at home. That was a big relief in case she was expected to do the driving sometimes!

There were many familiar things, but some strange ones too – chicken's feet, strange looking fish and moray eel were a couple of them!

But they managed to get everything they needed. Bread, milk, eggs, coffee, pasta, sandwich fillers, hot pepper sauce. That should keep them going.

They had decided to laze around on the pool and beach for their first day and have a BBQ later, so they added chicken thighs, steak, and hot pepper sauce to their purchases. Plus a bag of charcoal, matches and firelighters.

Finally they bought wine – 3 red and 3 white plus a case of the famous Bajan Banks beer. Perfect.

They checked out and stored their goodies in a cool box in the boot.

Adam decided that the sun was over the yardarm hours ago back in the UK, so on the way back he stopped at the Fisherman's Inn, not far away.

They sat at the plastic tables overlooking the beach and the ocean, sipping local beer from the bottle.

They had a look at the wonderful smelling food – Crab callaloo (a sort of carb and vegetable curry served in many Caribbean islands with many different variations), macaroni cheese which was more solid than they were used too, home fried chicken, peas and rice (which was actually kidney beans and rice), a pepper pot stew. All home cooked and set out in chafing dishes ready for serving.

They hadn't had any breakfast and decided they could do with something, so they ordered some chicken and some callaloo with a portion of peas and rice.

'How far removed could you get from Le Cinq where they had been dining last month was this', mused Rachel.

But it was every bit as delightful, in its own way. Watching the bright sun glistening on the water made eating the home cooked food very special.

Adam pointed things out to her.

"See that tree – the one with the red ring around?", he pointed. "The one with the little 'apples' on?".

She nodded.

"Well, that's a Manchineel tree. Don't go too near and definitely don't shelter underneath one if there's a tropical shower. The drops will cause nasty blisters on your skin. Steer well clear of 'em".

A few locals swam on the small beach to the side of the Inn. All beaches in Barbados were public beaches and anyone could visit them, locals and tourists alike.

Rachel was very fair and was glad to be sitting in the shade. The warm sun beat down. She put a little sun cream on to be safe – she didn't want her dream holiday spoiled by sunstroke.

By and by the couple reluctantly settled the bill and set about delivering their shopping back to the beach house.

Adam drove. They covered the few miles and soon the automatic gates were swinging open for them.

Rachel unpacked the shopping and Adam unloaded the beers and wine.

At last, they were all ready to do nothing

Adam told Rachel that he had to cover off his residency formalities in Bridgetown the next day, but it should only take an hour or so. He asked Rachel if she's like to come along and look round the shops while he was doing his business and she readily agreed. Bridgetown was a safe place for tourists if you didn't stray beyond certain boundaries. And there was some fantastic duty- free shopping to be had.

They went upstairs and changed into their swimwear. He in a pair of Lauren shorts and she into one of her new bikinis. They grabbed two towels and raced back downstairs.

Rachel was pleased with her bikini shopping. This one wasn't at all expensive, but she sure looked a million dollars in it. It was smaller than she normally chose. Not a thong – she hated those things – but very brief briefs. And her boobs almost spilled out of the top.

"Wow!" said Adam as she came into view.

Apart from both looking pale skinned and pasty, the couple looked every bit the tourists. They worked on getting a tan. Rachel used the sun cream regularly. She knew she needed protection, but she also liked the feel of Adam rubbing it gently into her back and her shoulders.

The marks on Rachel's bum could still be seen, but thankfully were very faint now. Thank goodness.

They sipped beer and began the books they had brought with them. This was heaven.

They slipped in and out of the swimming pool every so often to cool down. They played happily in the water. They took a walk on the dazzling beach. They paddled in the sea. They did everything that lovers do on their first day in paradise.

After a couple of hours, Rachel had to retreat to the shade, but Adam stayed out in the sun. He was lucky – he had an olive skin and tanned easily. Rachel's fair complexion meant that she turned tomato red if she overdid it. Still, she was happy with her book.

This was the life.

Time flew by and the heat began to go out of the sun.

"Are you hungry yet", asked Adam.

"Not ravenous, but I will be in an hour or so", said Rachel.

"OK, I'll start prepping the Barbie", said Adam.

"Let me, please", offered Rachel.

She got no argument and so she wrapped herself in a sarong and took herself off to the kitchen indoors.

She scored the chicken and rubbed it in hot pepper sauce. She put it in the fridge to marinate

She simply ground a little salt and pepper onto the lovely steaks and then covered them.

She boiled some water, salted it, and emptied the rice into it. They had had to make do with tinned kidney beans, so these 'peas' would be added later.

The wine was already chilling, but she put a couple of glasses in the freezer so it would be ice cold when served.

It gets dark around 6pm all year round in Barbados and it was already very dark now. The stars – millions of them – twinkled brightly. It was a balmy evening.

Adam lit the charcoal. "Give it 30 minutes and I'll start cooking he said.

Rachel turned off the nearly cooked rice and added the kidney beans.

He loaded the cooking grate with steak and chicken.

She re-warmed the rice by scalding it with boiling water and leaving it steeping.

Soon they were eating their delicious feast under the stars.

They drank chilled wine from iced glasses.

'Could we be more in love?' Rachel thought to herself dreamily. "Could it be more perfect?"

They made love twice that evening – slow and sensuous. They had a wonderful sense of well-being and slept like logs.

After a light breakfast, they set off towards Bridgetown for the government offices.

They pulled into a gas station for fuel – the Range Rover was distinctly low. As the attendant filled the tank, a full steel band struck up. They played lovely, carefree calypso music and the couple just stood and watched long after the petrol tank had been filled.

Mindful of his appointment, Adam dragged them away and they soon hit traffic on the way into the capital.

Rachel noticed that to bus stops all had 'To Town' written on them when you were travelling towards the capital. They had misjudged the traffic and there was no time to drop Rachel off for shopping in downtown Bridgetown. She went with him to his meeting in the dull concrete building which served as government offices.

They were just about on time, but the officers were not. Over half an hour late, Adam was called into the office. The residence permit formalities, though, were very quickly done and the couple were soon on their way 'to town'.

Adam pulled into one of the car parks just off the main shopping street. Having parked up, they walked the short distance back to Broad Street. It was a favourite shopping area for cruise ship visitors – hardly anything authentic Bajan, but good prices from the brand name stores. Better still he could sit on the balcony of 'The Nelson' sipping a beer whilst Rachel shopped!

He showed her the shops, handed her one of his credit cards and told her to buy something nice.

She went off and he duly placed himself upstairs at the pub, watching the world go by. Over his drink, he decided that tonight would be the night he asked Rachel to move in with him. He was expecting her to want to, as things had gone well so far.

In the bustle of the street below, he picked out Rachel once or twice, winding her way in and out of stores. Her blonde hair made her stand out from the crowd. Not that she wouldn't anyhow, he smiled to himself.

Eventually she waved to him from the street, bag in hand and then climbed the stairs to the Nelson's balcony.

Adam ordered her a chilled wine and asked her about her purchases. Turned out she had just bought a top she liked and a couple of Jill Walker trays for Ange.

Adam laughed. "No need to be careful", he said. "You can buy whatever you like". But Rachel wasn't like Adam. She was delighted with little, thoughtful purchases. She didn't need to spend big, particularly when it was someone else's money she was spending.

Eventually they strolled back to the car, hand in hand.

They drove back up the coast road to Holetown. Adam booked a Table at the Beach House for dinner. Not a flashy or hugely expensive place, but he had been before, and the food was tremendous.

"Kate Moss's parents used to own the place when it was a club, but they sold up a while ago", said Adam matter-of-factly.

They pulled up at a rum shack at the roadside and Adam allowed himself one more drink. The almost compulsory rum punch.

They were almost home now but Adam insisted on another stop at the Mullins Beach Bar.

"It used to be called Suga, Suga, but things are changing quickly on this coast", he said. "The smaller hotels are being swallowed up and turned into swanky apartments – nothing under a couple of million."

Sitting on the beach in Mullins Bay, watching the turquoise sea, sipping a coke. It was heaven in the warmth of the afternoon.

The sun set over the bay, the reflection sparkled orange on the water. After watching the last of the sunset, they sighed, got back in the car, and drove the short way home.

Rachel was a little tired and so they cancelled their dinner reservation and Adam called Winnie.

Adam had something on his mind, and they needed to talk with some degree of privacy, so it was probably for the best.

Winnie rushed out to the shops and bought the food which Adam said they would like for dinner. Fresh fish, salad, and new potatoes. And a cheeky dessert which she could choose for them.

She managed to get some thick Tuna steaks, fresh off the boat that morning. She got another couple of bottles of wine and more beer, plus a half bottle of Mount Gay rum. They could always drink that with Coke if they finished the rest, she reasoned.

Meanwhile, Rachel and Adam had changed, and they were in the pool. The water was still warm, despite it being dark. They put some logs on the barbecue. Not to cook anything, just to make a nice atmosphere.

As they swam, Adam said to Rachel, "I've got something I want to ask you, Rachel"

"OK, ask away", she replied shaking the pool water from her hair.

"Well, I love you first of all"

"I love you too, Adam"

"Well, you are spending quite a lot of time over at mine these days. We get on so well. What would you think about moving in with me?"

"Oh!", exclaimed a surprised Rachel. "That's taken me completely by surprise!. Could I have time to think about that, please Adam? I'm not saying no, but there are a few things worrying me. I need to get my thoughts in line and then we need to talk again. Is that OK?".

Adam was a little disappointed, but he tried not to show it.

"You take all the time you need", he replied. He had expected an 'Oh yes please!', type response and it had not been forthcoming.

Was something wrong?

Chapter Thirty-Two

The Conversation

For the rest of that evening, they ignored the elephant in the room. They swam a little and then ate Winnie's fabulous Tuna Steaks, complete with herb crust.

The surprise dessert was a bit of a mystery – pastry based, tropical fruit filled and cream on top. They had no idea what it was, but it was tasty, all the same.

Winnie loaded the dishwasher and took her leave. Adam tipped her well.

Adam and Rachel agreed to talk the next day when she had had a chance to get her head around the idea.

They showered and slipped into bed, the air conditioning taking the edge off the muggy night. This was rainy season in the Tropics and thunderstorms and high humidity were pretty standard.

Adam put his arms around her.

She snuggled into him.

Soon they were kissing.

They made slow, sensual love twice that night.

Adam was concerned and he needed the closeness.

Rachel was just randy.

The next morning, livened up in the sluicing shower and fortified by strong Jamaican coffee, they nibbled at pastries as they sat down at the table to talk.

"Can I start, please Adam?"

"I love you very much, but I have a few worries about upping and moving in with you, don't misunderstand me please, but I wouldn't be happy without discussing them with you".

"No, I understand. Please go on".

"Firstly, there's my flat. I am in the early days of a mortgage to buy it. My independence is important to me. If, down the line, we fall out – not that I think we will, but I must think like this – what would I do? I would have given up my job and my home and have nothing. I need a little more security than that".

"That makes perfect sense to me. What else is worrying you?"

Rachel noticed Adam jotting down brief notes.

"Ange. I do miss my friend. Not so much anyone or anything else, but she is someone I can go to for help and advice.".

"Hmmm", said Adam. "That one is a bit more difficult to solve. Let me think about that one".

"Next is money. I know you have been extraordinarily generous to me – my lovely car, Paris and now this. But sometimes it feels like – excuse me for saying this, but I'll say it anyhow – like prostitution of sorts. You give me nice things; I oblige in the bedroom. Or the Summer House", she added to lighten the conversation. "I feel a bit like a gold digger. That is not how it is, honestly. I think we need to clarify our relationship".

Adam looked stunned, but he kept writing. "That is most definitely not how I see it. I want to put that one to bed after you have finished talking".

"I'm shocked, but please go on".

"Thank you. There's one more thing. You have shown me many aspects of submissiveness. I have enjoyed them all. It's a question of degree, I guess. It's just that, on the occasions I have been taken to task, on a few occasions I have been left feeling I have been dealt with too severely. I am not trying to – what is the expression? - top from the bottom. It is just that I have been left barely able to walk a couple of times. It makes me feel worthless and unloved. Can we talk about this please? I love everything about you except this. And I know this a side of the relationship that you really enjoy – it might be a deal breaker, I know, but we have to talk."

Adam was even more stunned at this. Effectively he was being told he was just too severe, and he would need to tone it down for the future. He continued with his notes.

Rachel gave him back the talking stick.

"Well, I appreciate your honesty and your concerns. Let's try and address them one-by-one as I think of how I can make you feel more at ease, but the one I want to address straight away is making you compare your relationship with me to feeling like a prostitute.

I am devastated you feel like that. Even though I think it has come across stronger than you intended, I am so sorry you feel that way.

I love you Rachel, truly. I never ever intended to make you feel worthless and I'm really upset that I have".

Rachel could see small tears forming in his eyes. She rushed to him and held him. Those tears were all the answer she needed to that question. "Don't worry darling", she whispered. "We'll work out a good way forward". She kissed his forehead

Having gathered himself together, he went on earnestly, "When I buy you things it's because money means nothing to me. Even if I didn't work, I'd have the millions of pounds left to me by my parents. Since then, I have used my billions of pounds – and it is billions – as a way to make people happy. A pay rise here, a trip there. It isn't in return for anything. I just want to make people happy. And I had to come here in person to sort residence permits out, so why not ask the woman I love to come with me?"

"Now I know this sort of contradicts what I have just said, but how about this for a solution to the security issues if we don't work out? I pay off your remaining mortgage and the flat in Middlesex is then there for you to return to anytime. Nothing to do with me. And let's agree that this will be the last big thing I do for you unless we have spoken about it, and you have agreed?".

"You can't do that!"

"But I can. Easily. And I want to."

"I'll work on the other things, I promise, and propose some solutions quickly. I want you to be happy. Will you promise to think about the flat proposal? I am to have answers before we go home, OK?"

"OK. Thank you, Adam. I'm so glad we could talk like this about things. I'm feeling better already".

Adam sighed.

He hadn't seen that one coming.

Chapter Thirty-Three

The Rest of the Holiday

"Let's go on that island tour you promised me!", said Rachel the next morning. "We could take a picnic?"

"Great idea", replied Adam.

The couple nipped along to Jordan's and bought stuff for their picnic – sandwich loaf, cooked chicken drumsticks, sliced ham, fruit, cheese and more.

They made a mountainous picnic and threw it in the cool box, together with wine and beer. They were anxious to get on their way.

Rachel was determined that their conversation mustn't spoil the rest of the holiday – they still had a week and a half left to enjoy. Adam was a little quieter than usual, but other than that he seemed his normal self.

They set off in the Jeep which Adam kept in the garage. It had a top which clipped on but was otherwise open to the elements. A perfect way of exploring the island as it was useful for off-roading.

They set off north to Speightstown and turned right once they had passed through the town itself, heading for North Point and the animal flower cave.

Rachel was a bit underwhelmed by the sea anemones which were exposed in a cave at low water but loved the ruggedness of the Atlantic Ocean smashing over huge rocks. A complete contrast to the West Coast, she thought. They stayed a while and sat on the grass, watching the powerful waves break below.

The next port of call was to be Bathsheba with its famous 'Soup Bowl', known to surfers all over the world. The beaches on this side of the island were much less crowded. The sea was more dangerous. It had a kind of wild beauty. They stopped for a beer in one of the beach shacks.

Next stop was Bottom Bay. Parking was difficult and they had to clamber over a few rocks to get there, but what a sight greeted them. The bluest sea; the whitest beach. Strewn with coconut palms. Absolutely deserted. They decided to swim and had a wonderful time dodging the waves.

They explored the beach and found a cave at the far end. Adam chivalrously went back to the car to get the picnic. They would never find a better spot than this.

They set out their hamper near the entrance to the cave and enjoyed their picnic and a few drinks. After eating, they looked round the totally deserted sands. They swam again. And then flopped down on the edge of the sea.

Lust got the better of them and they made love slowly, with the waves lapping over their feet. Never had Rachel felt so peaceful.

Crane Bay – voted one of the World's top ten beaches was next, then on past the airport to St Lawrence. If Barbados had fleshpots, they would be at St Lawrence. It was pleasant, but an unsophisticated tourist trap with themed pubs and Sports bars. They decided not to stop there.

On past the fish markets of Oistins and curling round towards town and the south side of Bridgetown. Just short of the capital, they noticed a lot of cars. The racing was on today at Garrison Savannah.

Adam parked the car on a grass verge, and they joined the throng. Adam asked one of the locals what he was betting on in the next race and put ten dollars on it, He didn't hold out much hope, but bet it anyway…. And it won! At odds of 10 to 1. He collected his 110$ and looked for the man who gave him the tip. He wanted to buy the guy a beer, but he couldn't find him. They moved on through Bridgetown and onto the Coast Road back to Mullins.

It was late afternoon when they were able to wash the dust of the day's journey off in their pool.

The rest of the fortnight was spent just relaxing. The conversation they had had wasn't mentioned. They just enjoyed each other's company. They made love every day. They went to Welchman's Hall Gully and met the monkeys which roam there. They gathered nutmeg and mace to take home.

All too soon the fortnight was gone. They packed their cases and set out with the agency driver for the airport.

They sat in the cool of the airport lounge and boarded the aircraft when called.

It had been idyllic.

Almost all the time.

Chapter Thirty-Four

Angela and Jane Catch Up

It had been a while since Angela and Jane had last met. They agreed to meet for a coffee. Ange. was missing Rachel very much so she valued Jane's friendship

Jane walked into the coffee bar looking windswept. She was undoubtedly beautiful, thought Angela.

A beautiful face, nice hair, fantastic figure. But after a couple of meetings, their get togethers were getting a bit 'samey' for both girls.

They sipped at their lattes. Ange wiped the foam from her top lip before she asked a of Jane

"Can I ask you a question, Jane?".

She didn't wait for an answer.

"What exactly are you looking for from our meetings? Because I'm not at all clear".

"Yes, I've been thinking a lot about that. We can't just go on with doing the same things, else it will become boring. I think that I have already got what I wanted - should I say needed? - from our meetings.

I think now, I would like to try something similar with a man.". Stumbled over her words a little nervously.

"What, you mean you want to try some discipline from your boyfriend?" asked Ange.

"Oh God no!" replied Jane.

"With an authoritative stranger. My boyfriend wouldn't understand at all. He simply not into all this on any level", she explained.

"Ah, I see."

"I have enjoyed what we have tried together, and it has certainly taught me lots. But now I've clarified it in my head, I need to try it with a guy".

"Good for you", said Ange. She was also finding the same sort of routine, once a month, was becoming more than a little wearing.

"How do you plan to move forward with that, then?", said Angela.

"I don't know really", answered Jane. "I thought I might do what you did. Join a contact website which specialises in this sort of thing. You know – set up a profile and see what crops up.

I know I'll have to be very selective. I guess there are plenty of perverts on these sites, but you never know – I might get lucky."

Angela said she thought that was a reasonable plan. She even gave her the names of the websites she used.

"Thank you. That is really kind of you!", said Jane gratefully. "I very much appreciate that".

"No problem", replied Angela. "Please keep in touch though. I'd like to know how you get on and it might be fun to meet up from time to time. You never know what might happen!", said Ange.

"That's nice. I promise to keep you up-to-date with everything", replied Jane.

They parted firm friends.

They promised to stay in touch.

Ange doubted they would.

Chapter Thirty-Five

The Solutions for Rachel

After a lovely in-flight meal and a few drinks, the couple settled into their chosen movies, but before too long they were dozing.

They asked for their seats to be made into flat beds and – for a flight – they had a decent amount of sleep. Before they knew it, they were being gently woken for breakfast service.

Neither fancied too much to eat – it was still about 4am in their heads.

Soon they landed, a few minutes ahead of schedule.

They hurried through immigration and customs and were pleased to see Michael there, waiting for them.

He took over the pushing of the luggage trolley and led them back to the Bentley.

They didn't feel like too much chatter on the drive back home and Michael respected this, suggesting they had a quick snooze.

Very soon they were back in the lanes around Godstone. Markedly less leafy than when they had departed. It was a gusty day and the remainder of the leaves on the were fluttering down as Winter approached.

As they arrived home, neither were up for a chat – they were too tired. They went to bed, but Adam did say, before they drifted off, "Rachel, I've been busy. I have what I hope are solutions for you. Let's talk this evening when we feel a bit more human?"

"I'd like that", said Rachel.

They woke a few hours later and showered. Both felt refreshed.

Both were ready to try to find solutions to Rachel's concerns.

She had wisely booked an extra day off work and would be stopping with Adam that evening.

Let's open a nice wine while we talk, Adam suggested. So they did.

"May I go first?" asked Adam.

"Of course"

"OK, well I believe your points 1 and 3 are linked. You need the security of somewhere to go if things don't work out and would need a job if living in Godstone. However, you don't want to be made to feel like a charity case or, as you put it, a sort of prostitute" he started.

"That sums up a lot of it, yes", said Rachel.

He went to his computer. It took a while to boot up as it had been turned off for two weeks. While it started, he went on, "Please let me finish before you say anything, O.K. ?"

She nodded.

"If you moved in with me here, first, I would pay off your mortgage. The flat in Hillingdon would be legally yours. But I propose that you would pay me back at the same rate as your monthly mortgage is now. You could rent it out for around £1,500a month and that would mostly cover the repayment. So long as we are together you would be repaying me, but if you ever wanted us to split, the flat would still be yours".

"Anticipating your next question, how would I earn? What job could I do here in Surrey? I couldn't possibly commute to the Estate Agency. Am I right?"

She nodded again.

"Come and have a look at this", he said.

Adam walked her over to his PC, clicked a few buttons and a formatted advert appeared:

"Personal Assistant Required. Immediate start. Reporting directly to the proprietor, responsibilities would include organising travel and meetings, property management, handling insurances. Unusual working hours will apply on occasion. High organisational skills and smart appearance necessary. Some travel involved. Top salary paid for the right skill set, based on £65,000 p.a. Please reply to…."

Rachel was stunned. He was offering her a job. A well-paid job which she would be able to do. And security so that she would have a place to go if she needed it. And no charity. She wouldn't be a gold-digger – she'd be earning her keep. This sounded like a perfect arrangement.

"I had just advertised for a P.A. before we went way. Michael is good, but he is really a driver and in truth it was all getting a bit much for him. Even with the pay rise!. This is something which I genuinely need. It is not a charity thing – this is a real job for which you would be paid a very good salary. It is something I feel you could do very well for me."

"The job would entail, for example, liaising with the guys in Barbados to put them on standby for visits. Or with my pilot to organise availability for trips. Talking to clients to organise meetings. Making sure I was updated at the start of each week with all upcoming events. And at the start of each day, reminders. Genuine, important work. So tell me, have I put these worries to bed?"

Rachel tried to pick fault with the plan, but all in all Adam had it covered. It seemed a sound, equitable solution.

"Next was your friend Angela, I believe? I don't have a magic wand for this one, I must be honest. But I am away about 50% of the time. Sometimes I'll be able to justify a P.A. to come with me. Others you'll be left at home, kicking your heels. I'm happy for you to go over to Middlesex at these times, so long as you have the phone switched on.

In this way, you'll probably see MORE of her than you do now! And you have reliable transport too."

Rachel could see the sense in this too. The argument was annoyingly simple, but it worked. She nodded thoughtfully.

"O.K." she said. "That seems good".

"Next", Adam continued, "are the gifts and things. I have explained that money means nothing to me except as a way to make you happy. I have offered not to spend big money on you without agreement. Would that be OK? I'm sure I'll trip up on the odd occasion but does that sound better in principle?".

"Without a doubt. Thank you for understanding, Adam", said Rachel.

"Then I think that leaves us with one issue. The elephant in the room. Sometimes you think you have been dealt with too severely. I won't lie about this one, hard punishment is – when deserved – one of the things which keeps me most interested.

I'm still thinking about this one, but we could try a safe word which, if you use it at the point it is getting too much, would stop the punishment. But it would be continued the next day? Or I could split all severe punishments into two sessions, spaced apart by a day or so? Or I could substitute a severe punishment with half a dozen spankings?

Would you give this some more thought please? I will too. The important thing is that we talk".

"I agree", said Rachel. "For my part I know I won't do everything right. I know I will be punished. Sometimes hard. I welcome that and hope that I'll make you happy by submitting to it. But never so hard I can't walk. That is brutal in my eyes. I start doubting if you love me when you hurt me that much".

"I understand darling. I honestly do".

In the conversations that followed, Adam agreed to go slightly easier on Rachel when administering her punishments.

And Rachel asked for a few more days to consider his solutions.

She decided that all in all, she was happy and phoned Adam with the news.

He was delighted.

"Right, we'll do things properly", Adam responded. "First, if you can get copies of your mortgagor and find out if there any penalties for early settlement and let me have that, I'll set the wheels in motion to pay it off. Ask them for the settlement amount.

Secondly, I will get you a formal job offer letter out with a contract of employment, so you are covered. What notice period are you on? When would you want to start?"

"I'm on a month's notice, so maybe early to mid-December?", said Rachel.

"I'll set everything in motion this week", promised Adam.

"Don't resign from you current job until your mortgage is paid and you have accepted the Job Offer", said Adam.

"OK darling. Can I tell Ange?"

"Of course. Why not."

"Fantastic. Thank you Adam. I love you darling".

"Love you more", he joked back.

Seemed like they were back on track again.

A huge relief for Rachel.

Chapter Thirty-Six

The Nitty Gritty

Adam was as good as his word.

Rachel had phoned the mortgage company and got a settlement figure. She passed on the amount for early settlement – a shade over £210,000. This was passed on to Adam and in turn his solicitor.

The mortgage company send out paperwork for Rachel to sign which she did and passed on to the solicitor. In a matter of days, she was mortgage free – a wonderful situation to be in at her age!

Adam also posted her a formal letter from his main company, offering her the position as his Personal Assistant.

The salary was to be a little more than the promised £65k. The letter stated £72k, which would work out at £6k per month. She could add rental income to this in due course and she would easily be able to afford to make repayments to Adam as promised.

The accompanying contract of employment was given the once over by his solicitor. The only comment he had to make was the six-months' notice period on the company's part (one-month on Rachel's part) was unusual and perhaps over-generous, but Adam had done this on purpose to provide her with some security.

Rachel was delighted. This was more than double her estate agent's salary and she felt she could pay her way.

She signed the letter and returned it the same day.

She phoned Adam to tell him so.

He had ordered her a company Gold Amex card for expenses. She felt important!

The only thing they had to do was arrange a start date. They decided on early January, which would allow Rachel to work her notice and to get her flat ready for rental and to make the move.

Everything was agreed and she couldn't wait.

Rachel rang Ange. and arranged drinks for the following Thursday evening. "I have so much to tell you, Ange. It's big, exciting news. But I'm not telling you what it is until we meet".

Ange had strongly protested, but Rachel just wouldn't tell her, so she'd just have to wait.

"Not fair", Ange grumped.

"Don't care", Rachel laughed.

Not one to hang about, Rachel started painting those rooms which needed it in the evenings. From her time at the agency, she knew exactly how to dress properties for widest appeal. Neutral colours. Minimal furniture. Tidy garden. And she cleared out loads of clutter which made the flat look smaller. She cleared out the garage too. Off street parking would help her let the place, she knew.

Adam agreed that it was O.K. to hand in her notice now, which meant she would actually finish work on the first week in December. Perfect.

So Rachel typed a formal letter of resignation. She felt awkward, having been at the Estate Agency for six years, but they were very nice to her. Told her how much they would miss her and thanked her for her efforts.

Rachel also told them that she would have a flat to let and asked if the agency would like to handle the letting. A nice touch, with which they were very pleased. She was leaving them on the best of terms.

Thursday came and after work Rachel rushed home, showered, and changed. She walked round to the pub and went in via the side door.

Angela was already in there, waiting eagerly for the big news.

"Right!", she said. "Spill the beans! And this better be BIG news. I've been excited ever since you told me. Well?".

"Hang on a minute! Let me get a drink first!", she moaned. "What would you like?".

Both girls decided on a large Gin and Tonic. With ice and a slice.

Rachel went to the bar and ordered them. She took them back to the table and set them down before beginning to talk.

"Well, the big news is I'm moving in with Adam!", started Rachel.

She saw a flicker of doubt in her friend's eyes. After all, they had only known each other less than a year – quite a bit less!

But when she explained the security he had provided, Ange's worries for her friend disappeared.

"Wow!", she exclaimed. "You must've made a hell of an impression Rach! But what will you do for work though?".

Rachel brandished a copy of her employment offer and passed it to her friend.

"Bloody hell! £72,000 a year? Six months notice? BUPA, Pension? You really can't go wrong with this", she said as she studied the letter. "Good for you Rachel. You deserve this".

She was pleased for her best friend.

"But what about us? We'll never see each other!!!"

Rachel explained that, with Adam away on business so much, he was quite happy for her to be out and about, so long as she had the phone with her and switched on. She would actually have MORE time to see Ange!".

"I've changed my mind", said Ange. "Please tell Adam that I WILL meet with him after all!".

Both girls laughed out loud.

It could so easily have been Ange thought Rachel.

The conversation moved on to the Barbados holiday.

Looking back, it had been almost perfect.

Rachel told Angela about the house, the car, the weather, the scenery, the picnics and barbecues, the lovely people. She even told her about making love with the sea lapping round them

"Oh, and I won't be seeing Jane any more", said Ange. "She decided to try her luck with men. In truth it was all getting a bit samey. She decided she needed to try a dominant male, so good luck to her. She'll need to very careful though. I warned her of that."

"Yes, definitely. There seem to be loads of weirdos out there."

It was a school-day tomorrow, so they drained their glasses and walked home.

"Your garden looks nice", remarked Ange.

"I would hope so", said Rachel. "It took me five hours work to tidy that up!"

It was only when she got indoors that she realised they had not even touched on the Caribbean holiday once.

Oh well, there would be plenty of other times, she was sure of that.

Chapter Thirty-Seven

Tying up Loose Ends

Rachel worked her months' notice and handed over all her properties to colleagues. She was determined to leave professionally and worked hard at doing so.

She finished redecorating the flat. It looked lovely in the photos she took for the Estate Agency. They quickly turned the pictures into full property details and began advertising the place, to be available from the first week in January.

It was advertised at the same rate as a 2 bedroomed flat in the same road, although Rachel was convinced that hers looked much nicer. It had off road parking too. That must be worth something.

She continued going over to Adams most weekends on a Friday. Whenever she visited, she packed a load of her clothes with her.

Adam had thoughtfully prepared one of the bedrooms as a pre-moving in room. It had loads of space. Bit by bit, she moved her clothes and a few other possessions into the Surrey house. She was going to let her flat as furnished and so had no big white goods to worry about. And she could easily move clothes from the pre-moving in room to their bedroom once she had decided what she wanted on a daily basis.

Adam had been completely supportive, keeping true to his word on every aspect of their 'deal'.

It was one of those Fridays today, and Rachel arrived at the house. The Mini was laden with clothes and shoes.

Adam came outside and hugged her, then helped her in and upstairs with her load. It took four or five trips. Who'd have believed a Mini would hold that much!

Rachel felt like she should have thrown some of these clothes away. Many were comfy old favourites and probably past their best.

They decided on Thai food for their Friday night takeaway, so Adam phoned the order, to be delivered for 8:30.

The couple talked about the week they had had. Rachel handing over stuff. Adam clinching yet another big deal. Things were going well.

Adam asked how Angela had taken the news.

"Very positively. She is delighted for us both", Rachel answered honestly. Adding "She is a really nice person."

They ate their meal and watched television for an hour or two before bed. Something detectivey, but they couldn't even remember the name.

They went up to bed. Adam followed Rachel, admiring the view.

When they got to the bedroom, Adam asked her if she had misbehaved since he last saw her.

Taken by surprise, she stuttered over her reply.

"I'm not sure really. I've been so busy"

She looked directly at Adam. "But I haven't been spanked for a while. I think you should probably give me a reminder?", she smiled flirtatiously.

"Yes" was the simple reply.

He cleared the dressing table with one sweep of his forearm and firmly bent her over the edge of it.

She was wearing a short silk robe. He slowly slid it up over her bottom, revealing white lacy briefs underneath. He spanked her quite hard and quite long. She closed her eyes and enjoyed the sensation as Adam covered every inch. First he spanked her over her pants and then he bared her bottom and covered every inch again. Sure it stung, but it was sensuous, and she had to admit, she loved it.

And now she wanted fucking. Hard.

Adam somehow knew and was happy to oblige.

He went at it without hesitation and slipped his penis inside her.

"And now I'm going to fuck your brains out", he said.

And he very nearly did.

Both satisfied, they slipped into the huge bed and quickly fell asleep.

The next morning, Saturday, they decided to go somewhere for the day, but they couldn't decide exactly where.

"I've got it!", exclaimed Rachel. "Let's go to Hastings and eat fish and chips! I'll drive!", she enthused.

And so they found themselves sitting on the sea wall in Hastings, eating the best fish and chips in town. Avoiding the annoying sea gulls, who would do anything, it seemed, to nick one of them. They had even found a public car charging point on the front, just to make sure.

They had a pint in the dodgy looking Hastings pub. Well, Adam did. Rachel stayed on the soft drinks because of driving home. She was being good today.

It wasn't sitting outside weather, so they went inside the dubious pub. One drink was enough, they decided.

And they set off for home soon afterwards.

On a whim, they stopped at a pub just outside Royal Tonbridge Wells. This was much mor like it. It would have been a good place for a meal if they weren't stuffed with fish and chips! Never mind. They had a couple more drinks and continued their journey home.

Once the Mini was safely back on charge, Rachel said "Please get me a drink darling! I've been so good all day and I am gasping!".

Adam disappeared and cam back with two huge glasses of white wine. Chilled to perfection.

"What a fun day", said Adam. "And the Mini goes really well, doesn't it?. Let's do this again!".

"Absolutely. It's been brilliant!" said Rachel.

They woke on the Sunday to weak Winter sunshine and decided to walk to the pub for their lunch. Rachel had enjoyed the Hare and Hounds, so they went back there.

The warm interior of the pub was welcome after the briskness of outside.

They chose their food, read the Sunday papers, and smiled at the people who recognised them.

Again the pub-grub was fantastic. It shouldn't be called pub grub, Rachel decided. Pub grub was pie and chips or gammon steak with pineapple or pizza. This was another level.

There was a log fire.

There was some sort of game where you swung a quoit of a string; trying to land it on the bull's horn. It was harder than it looked!

They walked back to the house, hand in hand and happy. As they entered the warmth of the house. Rachel wondered, could she be happier?

She decided she couldn't.

Adam and Rachel spent the rest of their weekend together doing nothing very much, and soon it was time for the drive back to Hillingdon.

It was to be her last week at work next week. She was taking colleagues out for a drink on the Friday, so she wouldn't be able to go over to see Adam on the Friday evening. They decided they would not see each other, and Rachel would pop over in the following week

Adam checked his work diary. He showed Rachel how it was organised, as soon she would be the one who organised it for him.

Simple enough, she thought.

She felt like this was a job she could easily do for Adam.

She would be the perfect P.A.

Rachel left for Hillingdon after Adam confirmed she would be able to come to see him at anytime in the week after she left work.

There was an accident on the M25 which caused traffic problems. She was delayed by the best part of an hour, but eventually pulled into her garage and put the Mini on charge.

She went indoors and put the kettle on.

Chapter Thirty-Eight

Rachel Leaves Work

Rachel had handed over most of her work and properties to chosen colleagues now and she didn't have a lot left to occupy her time.

She was mostly dealing with walk-ins and phone enquiries.

One of her team told her there had been an enquiry on her flat over the weekend. The couple would like a viewing sometime this week. They were apparently new to the area but decided that Hillingdon was within their budget.

The husband had a new job at Heathrow airport, so the location was perfect.

Rachel thought it would be strange if she showed them round herself and so asked if a someone else could show them round. The viewing was arranged for Wednesday at six-thirty, so before she went to work that day, she carefully tidied up and put fresh flowers around the place.

Apparently the viewing went well, and the couple were keen, but that would have to wait and see if that translated into a concrete offer.

And by the time they had looked round, Rachel had four more requests for a viewing. The apartment was p for rent at £1,250 per calendar month and was generating a lot of interest at that price.

The viewings were arranged, and it seemed some of the viewers were seriously tempted.

Hmmmm. Let's wait and see thought Rachel.

She had arranged after work drinks and sandwiches at a pub near her office for the Friday she left. Just for an hour or so.

And they had a collection for her. Rachel was very popular in the estate agency, and they had collected a good amount of money.

They closed a little early on that Friday, strolling down to the pub with Rachel. Rach had put money behind the bar – enough for two or three drinks each.

It was a nice goodbye. Her boss clinked his glass with a fork and made a short speech.

How valued she had been

How she had been a big success within the estate agency team

How lovely it had been working with her.

Wishing her luck in her new role.

Rachel responded to say how she would miss everyone and to wish them luck too

They presented her with some lovely crystal glassware, drank their drinks and one by one filtered out to start their weekend.

Rachel was the last to leave.

She looked around.

She liked this little place, and she really would miss her friends and work colleagues.

There weren't many people in the pub now.

As she stepped out to go home, she was a little sad.

Things would never be the same again, she thought, wistfully.

But she forced herself to think about what the future held in store for her.

A new job with lots of money.

She now owned her flat outright.

She could look forward to nice holidays.

And deliciously naughty sex.

She smiled. She was going to be OK!

Rachel went home and showered the London grime out her hair. She put on a robe and slippers and settled in for a night of television.

And good news followed the next day. The first couple to view the flat – the ones working at the airport – wanted to rent her apartment. The agency was just checking references. They would then take the deposit, draw up the contract and arrange a date for them to move in!

How quickly things were moving!

She phoned Adam, but as luck would have it he wasn't in, and she got the answerphone. Maybe he'd got a business meeting, she reasoned. In any case, he didn't want to be disturbed and she respected that. She left him a message with the great news about her flat. She would be able to start paying him back from day one, something which was very important to her.

So she curled up with the remote control and watched whatever she fancied.

It was nice to have a night to herself, but she really missed being with Adam.

Still, it wouldn't be long now, she thought to herself with a smile.

Not long at all.

Chapter Thirty-Nine

Jane gets a Match

Jane had spent a few days concocting her profile for the website.

She took numerous selfies which showed off her great figure but didn't show her face. She didn't want anyone she knew stumbling across her picture on a site like this!

She was very careful about what information she gave away. There were no suggestive photo's; no specific details about exactly what she was looking for. She hoped it would be tempting to someone. After all, she was a genuine beautiful girl. On a site like this there were very few genuine females, let alone ones who looked as good as her.

After chopping and changing little details, she decided it was time to plunge into the water.

She posted her profile and picture and got it approved.

'Let's see what replies I get.". She thought.

She had listened carefully to Ange's advice. She would do a phone check very early in the proceedings to make sure she was comfortable with the guy. She would quickly discard replies from females, potential perverts, etc.

She would consider the age ranges and rule out any too old or too young.

She would rule out married men.

And those who lived too far away to be practical.

And those without a photo.

And those who weren't handsome!

Over the next weeks, replies poured in.

She whittled them right down and was only left with two possible, so she let the process run for longer. This wasn't proving as easy as she had thought. She was getting lots of replies, but almost all of them were unsuitable.

Jane decided to sharpen up her profile to say exactly what she wanted and try again. She was much more specific. She added a photo of her bending over, showing off her bottom to good effect.

This time the replies were almost unmanageable!

She whittled them down to ten possible and then set about ranking these from one-to-ten.

She ran down the list. Numbers One and Two just sounded a bit master/slavey for her tastes and so were quickly rejected. Number Three sounded a little bit perverted.

But number four, a guy called David Taylor, sounded a distinct possibility.

He sounded self-assured and confident. Apparently he had lots of experience dispensing discipline to those who wanted or needed it.

The two built something of a bond in phone calls over the next few weeks and decided it was worth meeting. First meets should always be in always in a public place, Ange had advised her. That way you can always get up and leave if you don't feel comfortable. Good advice.

So they chose a Cuban restaurant in Islington for dinner and their first meeting.

Jane had had a tidy-up trim at the hairdressers and put on a little make-up. She picked a dress she thought was about right. Dressy with a hint of slut.

Despite having talked to David quite a few times on the phone, Jane was extremely nervous.

She looked in through the window – there was only one guy sitting on his own – he must be David.

Mustering all her courage, she opened the restaurant door and walked boldly up to the lone gent, smiling.

"David? David Taylor?", she asked nervously.

"Well", said the man, standing up and offering a half hug. "That's a name that I sometimes use for profiles on websites, so that I'm not recognised", he said, smiling.

"My real name is Adam." Admitted the handsome stranger "Adam De Vere".

Look out for the second book in this series from the same author:

"Rachel and Adam – Betrayal"

It is currently in writing and should be available in late 2022.